THE TURBULENT BISHOP

THE
TURBULENT
BISHOP

Radu Herklots

Troubador Publishing Ltd
Unit E2 Airfield Business Park,
Harrison Road, Market Harborough,
Leicestershire. LE16 7UL
Tel: 0116 2792299
Email: books@troubador.co.uk
Web: www.troubador.co.uk/matador

ISBN 978 1805141 327

British Library Cataloguing in Publication Data.
A catalogue record for this book is available from the British Library.

Printed and bound in Great Britain by 4edge Limited
Typeset in 11pt Adobe Garamond Pro by Troubador Publishing Ltd, Leicester, UK

Matador is an imprint of Troubador Publishing Ltd

This book is dedicated to the memory of my father.
Reverend Canon John Herklots

The Soaked by the Spirit Festival, Somerset

> *"It's all right, it's okay.*
> *Jesus loves you all the way*
> *Day or night, it's all right*
> *Jesus gonna show you the light".*

Robin Arbiter, organist of Rhyminster Cathedral, who had been invited to the largest evangelical event in the south-west to observe some more 'relatable' forms of worship, found it hard not to recoil.

Stanford in G and the cathedral's magnificent Father Willis organ this most certainly wasn't.

Although the trite words of the anthems were shown on massive screens, with a bouncing ball following the tune, everyone in the vast congregation already seemed to be familiar with them as they bopped up and down, arms outstretched in some kind of spiritual ecstasy.

To calm himself, Robin tried to imagine being back in his familiar stall in the quire during evensong, but the din was too loud.

In theory he welcomed the idea of a broad palette of worship, but this garbage? And just why did it seem so popular?

As they finished the 'Jesus loves you' number, a stage manager whispered an urgent message to Ben, the lead singer of the worship band: the keynote preacher had been delayed.

Ben made some kind of signal to the three other band members and they swiftly responded by bursting into an impromptu encore, which threatened to induce an outbreak of speaking in tongues among the fevered worshippers.

The disco-infused '*Sing Alleluia to Jesus*' struck the mild mannered organist as, if anything, even more of an offence to his liturgical sensibilities than the previous number.

The band – two guys, two girls – resembled a weedy Christian version of a manufactured UK Eurovision entry from the 1980s.

> "*Sing Alleluia to Jesus,*
> *Just let his love say hello*
> *Sing Alleluia to Jesus*
> *Yeah he loves to boogie*
> *And God is the sure way to go.*"

*

The keynote preacher was going to be delayed indefinitely. Security had found him lying in his yurt, face down.

It looked like he had been expertly knifed, but someone had also carved a huge letter 'A' on his back from which blood appeared to be seeping – and it was not just any old letter 'A'.

This was like something from a medieval manuscript, and it would have required hours of painstaking work to etch it on to the body.

ONE

Rhyminster, one year earlier

Plenty of water has flowed from the River Rhyme to the sea since we left John Tedesco and his faithful terrier, Barker, walking home across Cathedral Green after Bishop Bob's farewell party at the North Canonry.

As the lawyer turned detective said at the time, the bishop and his wonderful wife, Hilary, would be sorely missed; he could never have guessed how much, or by so many people.

We find Tedesco at a low ebb. Looking at himself in the mirror, he begins to see his father, and clothes that looked fine in the shop or on the screen seemed to develop a lived-in look as soon as he tried them on.

To add to his woes, his old affliction, imposter syndrome, has returned to haunt him. He remembers how he felt when he first qualified as a lawyer, being terrified of being found out if he momentarily forgot that his evening meal was called 'dinner' not 'tea', or if he referred to 'them' people instead of 'those'.

His comfortable world has changed and rather than a kind, gradual evolution, the process has been rapid and harsh.

Lynne Davey, his business partner, for whom he has repressed his feelings for too long, is sharing her life with Duncan Chivers of BBC *Searchlight*.

Much as Tedesco approves of the self-declared Alan Partridge of the south-west, he feels more than a tinge of envy.

Lynne spends alternate weekends at Duncan's apartment just off Plymouth Hoe, while he visits her terraced house in Rhyminster on the other ones.

"She's going to leave me, isn't she, Barker? They will move away, buy a lovely house together, and I'll be on my own."

Barker jumped on to his lap as if to say that he would always be there.

But Tedesco fretted about his canine pal. Barker was seven years old now, well into dog middle-age, and to add to his woes, his PA, Sally, seemed to have decided that she was in with a chance with her boss now that Lynne was 'spoken for'.

"You must have noticed, John," Lynne had said. "Since when did Sally Munks wear heels, spray perfume, spend ages checking her mascara?"

He, of course, had been oblivious, at least until Christmas, when a couple of glasses of amontillado had emboldened Sally into making her move, causing Tedesco to fall down the helter-skelter of a staircase at 4A Minster Precincts as he made his escape, lucky to get away with some nasty bruising.

Work provided little solace. He didn't want any more sensational murder cases, but something more interesting than tailing errant husbands and helping Lynne with her lucrative corporate recruitment work would be good. He felt like he was living in perpetual January.

However, it was the bigger Rhyminster scene that was really getting him down. Perhaps it was time to close the agency, move away and start again. Bishop Bob's new life in North Yorkshire seemed idyllic.

After he and Barker had stayed up there with Bob and Hilary for the first time, a couple of months later they found themselves house-sitting in Helmsley while the former bishop and his wife were in Scotland. Could this most Devonian of men settle in the North? He was beginning to think that he could.

What was it that was keeping him in Rhyminster? Change was all around him. Raj Purbani had managed to hold the parliamentary seat for the Conservatives despite the scandal of the selection contest, which led to the death of the leading candidate, and Barry Gulliver had resigned from the party in disgust, threatening revenge.

His vengeance amounted to reinventing himself as a most unlikely Liberal Democrat, winning a seat on the local council and embracing pavement politics. He was confident of being selected for the next general election, when he would try to take the seat from Purbani, who was already at home on the government benches and was being touted as a future leader.

Over at Tedesco's beloved cathedral poor Dean Dan had fallen out with the new bishop, who in a few short months had managed to wreak havoc upon one of the happiest dioceses in the Church of England. Tedesco's friend Canon Wilfred was tearing out what little remained of his hair.

The only good thing about the new bishop, known throughout the diocese as 'Jim Il Sung', was that the Master of Musick, having insulted him in public, had been suspended pending a capability procedure. Could Tantum be off at last?

No, Tedesco decided, the only thing that is keeping me here is Nicky.

His sister's long but turbulent marriage to Jeremy 'Chag' Wills had entered its final death throes and he couldn't abandon her, or his nephew and niece, Jack and Ella.

This wasn't going to be some new age 'conscious uncoupling', nor was it like a 60's jukebox tearjerker. Nicky and Chag were a bit long in the tooth for the teenage angst of 'Tears on my pillow' or 'Breaking up is hard to do'.

"Come on, Barker," he said. "Let's go to Jenks for some lunch. At least Joan isn't thinking of retiring."

TWO

The 79th Bishop of Rhyminster

So, how did it come to pass that the peaceful diocese of Rhyminster, which was reflected back to itself by the calm but authoritative style of Robert Dwyer, found itself turned on its head by the appointment of the new man?

As soon as Bishop Bob announced his retirement, a single question had dominated the Close and its environs: 'Who will be the new bishop?'

Hopes were high that it would be a woman. Rhyminster, despite its liberal brand of Anglicanism, was still far too male and stale.

Bishop Bob's protégé, Sarah Dillon, was an early bookies' favourite, as was Jane Le Prevost, the high-profile Dean of Salisbury.

Pete Leiper, the suffragan Bishop of Dartmoor – 'suffragan' loosely translates into secular as junior bishop – was keeping the plates spinning but in parishes throughout the diocese the natives were getting restless.

"When are we going to hear anything?" "Why does it take so long?" "Why can't they just appoint Pete? He's doing a good job."

It wasn't like this in the pages of *The Warden* or *Barchester Towers* when ecclesiastical appointments seemed to happen overnight.

These days a lengthy period of consultation and discernment took place and eventually a name would be put forward to the monarch.

As Canon Wilfred patiently explained to his friend John Tedesco, the key body in this byzantine process was the Crown Nominations Commission (CNC).

"I am really worried this time," said Wilf. "The evangelicals could pack the CNC and impose one of their own. Think about this as being like when Corbyn and his followers infiltrated the Labour Party."

Tedesco stroked his non-existent beard.

"Not the most reassuring comparison, is it? But this is the C of E – surely it isn't as factional as a political party?"

"Don't you believe it," Wilf replied. "The evo tendency – which is how we old-timers refer to the guitar-wielding evangelicals – is in the ascendancy, and it's the only part of the church which people think connects to the young. The archbishop seems to have accepted that this is the way forward, which means more informal worship and maybe the replacement of the parish system in its entirety."

"I don't like the sound of that," said Tedesco. "Does this mean worship bands instead of the choir? Drum 'n' bass instead of the organ?"

"I wouldn't joke about it if I were you, John. Dark days are coming, I fear. We will all have to pray hard that the Holy Spirit will direct the CNC in the right way."

*

And so, after machinations, deliberations, rumour and intrigue, the news was bruited abroad that James Provan was to be unveiled as the 79th Bishop of Rhyminster, bringing to an end a period of gestation that was long even by the standards of the established Church.

Rather than the new bishop being introduced to the press brandishing a team shirt with '79' on the back, as would have befitted a new striker for Rhyminster FC, a hastily assembled press conference was put together on a local beach, a location no doubt chosen for a variety of symbolic reasons.

BBC *Searchlight*, naturally, covered the event and star reporter Nicola Tedesco bagged the first interview with the bishop elect – he hadn't been a bishop elsewhere so would need to be consecrated, which normally took place in St Paul's or Westminster Abbey, before being formally installed in Rhyminster Cathedral.

"So, what will we call you?" Nicky breezily asked. "Bishop Jim?"

James Provan cut an imposing, even domineering, figure. At well over six feet he must have been the tallest bishop in the history of the diocese. There was not an ounce of fat on him, and he had a full head of jet black hair and piercing, somewhat sinister, green eyes.

He glared at his interviewer from a height. "Bishop James."

Trying to keep the mood light, Nicky tried another tack.

"Are you and your family looking forward to the move down here? Having lived in Devon all my life, I can tell you that this is a lovely area."

"I am not here to enjoy the scenery, Miss Tedesco," the new man stated, with a bluntness that took all who were listening by surprise.

"Neither am I here to make friends. I have been sent to this outpost of the kingdom to save souls and to go out and spread the word of God. From what I have seen of this part of the world, there is an air of complacency and a stubborn resistance to change which the Lord has sent me to challenge."

A flummoxed Nicky, not a description that would normally fit the experienced reporter, struggled to find the appropriate words with which to wrap up.

"Well, Bishop James, I can tell that everyone in the diocese is super excited by your appointment, and I look forward to talking to you again when you have moved down here later in the year."

THREE

Easter Sunday at Rhyminster Cathedral meant a bonkers o'clock start for the worshippers at the 5am service. The dawn liturgy commenced with the ceremonial bonfire on the west lawn, which always struck Tedesco, somewhat irreverently, as being like a scene straight out of *The Wicker Man*.

After a service of sufficient beauty and depth to challenge the most hardened atheist, the worship was followed by a joyful gathering in the cloisters with a glass of fizz to celebrate the Resurrection.

There was a palpable party atmosphere in the air, due in no small part to the hour, assisted on its way by the unaccustomed taste of early morning Lidl prosecco.

However, bubbling beneath the merry hubbub, the talk was all about the impending arrival of Bishop James.

Tedesco did his 'Che from *Evita*' thing, hiding behind columns so he could listen in to fragments of conversation.

"This will be the last time we do this!" boomed the Master of Musick, Charles Tantum.

"He wants a *worship band* at the Installation, whatever

that is, and, even worse, a *beatboxer*! I have let the dean know – over my dead body! He will have Elgar and Tallis or I'm off to Rome!"

Moving silently to lurk behind a pillar near the Chapter House, the detective overheard the unmistakable cut-glass voice of Lady Fiona Derrington.

"His wife sounds very demanding. I gather that she wants to completely redecorate the North Canonry, at vast expense, and that he wants to reorder the chapel!"

"I think he might be just what the Church needs," opined Commander Foster.

"A kick up the backside, no more woolly thinking."

"We certainly won't get any woolly thinking from James Provan," said the dean.

Wilf Drake had patiently explained to Tedesco that Provan was the nightmare choice as bishop, a complete break from the past and not in a good way.

"He studied at Moore College – what more of a clue did we need?"

"Sorry, Wilf. No idea what you are on about."

"My fault, John. Let me explain. Moore College is a training college in the Diocese of Sydney. The churchmanship there is the opposite of what we are used to here. The priests don't wear robes, they wear business suits, and if Provan has drunk from the Sydney fountain, then we may have an anti-woman bishop on our hands."

"But that's ridiculous, Wilf. He won't fit in at all."

"That's what the dean thinks. Although Dan came to us from the evo camp, he has gone native. He appreciates that a well-run cathedral with a proud choral tradition forms an important element in the Anglican blend. There should be room for worship bands as well as chamber music – we are a broad church after all."

"It doesn't sound as if Bishop James would agree with you, Wilf."

"That's what we are all afraid of…"

FOUR

Having wished a happy Easter to, amongst others, Sir Vere Alston (the former member of parliament), Jo Luxmoore (the dean's wife) and Lady Fiona, Tedesco wandered back through the Close to his cosy bolthole in St Budeaux Place, nestled just outside the Close but within its ancient 'liberty'.

He and Barker were going to his sister for Easter lunch and would be staying the night, but they wouldn't need to set off for a good couple of hours.

Having let himself in, Tedesco brewed a pot of coffee and dozed off until it was time for the paper shop to open.

"Come on, Barker, woof time!"

Barker looked up at his master with a quizzical expression, which gave the distinct impression that he hadn't been thrilled by Tedesco's early start, nor his perky air at such an hour.

The sun was just appearing over the little bridge, which, the detective reminded himself, was where Anthony Trollope had stopped to ponder one evening before his inspirational walk through the cathedral cloisters.

Barker was pondering something else entirely and found a familiar tree against which to complete his ablutions.

Having secured his Sunday paper and wished Agata, the new Polish owner of the shop, a happy Easter, the detective led his best mate back to base, where they both slouched and slumbered until noon, when Tedesco packed his little overnight Livingstone bag then gently bundled Barker into the back of the Lancia.

The traffic was surprisingly quiet; he assumed that this was due to the annual mass exodus abroad, which he found puzzling as this was his favourite time of the English year, a season that seemed to pass all too quickly after the drag of winter.

He had already lined up his musical accompaniment, another neglected piece by the most underrated songwriter in the history of these islands – at least in his opinion.

Clifford T Ward: '*April*'.

"There must be a 'Clifford T' revival one day, surely, Barker?"

He drove through Lower Woolford, crossed the river to the more aspirational upper side, then carefully steered the car through the five-barred gate of Crane House, realising a little late that he was more than slightly dreading the visit.

Whilst relieved to hear that his unbearable brother-in-law would be spending the holiday in the Maldives with his new, much younger partner, he knew that Nicky would want to discuss the legal aspects of her impending divorce with him – probably just as he was feeling like an early night and after too much alcohol.

To add to his apprehension, his nephew Jack was now at 'uni', which it certainly wasn't called in his day, and had become a full-blown Ayn Rand libertarian. Why couldn't he be a Marxist, or an eco-warrior, like normal students?

So, he would have to avoid discussing marriage and politics: that left religion. He would be fascinated to know what Nicky had really made of the new bishop.

As it turned out, he needn't have been apprehensive – the years seemed to roll back as his arrival, and especially that of Barker, was greeted with the same joyful enthusiasm as it had been when he had first brought his beloved pet to meet his new friends as a puppy.

Jack seemed way more interested in throwing a tennis ball for the terrier to retrieve than in trying to convert his uncle to an alt-right Liz Truss worldview, and Ella, now in the sixth form at South Devon, was eager to tell him about her plans to study for a degree in regenerative economics at nearby Dartington College.

His sister, however, was looking wiped out – if anyone deserved a break in the Maldives it was her. He had been amazed by how she had managed to show absolutely no hint of the pressures in her personal life when she appeared on the telly but seeing her for real he was instantly concerned.

Her ritual warm bear hug of a greeting seemed to linger forever before he managed to extricate himself.

"Something smells good, sis."

"It's rib of beef, from an organic farm near Totnes."

"Of course it is. And you will not be surprised to learn that I have raided Jos Elsted's cellar for something special to go with it."

The family lunch was a delight – this was what Tedesco had always hoped for and, although he hadn't been blessed with children of his own, he loved being an uncle.

After a communal washing-up session, during which he was constantly berated for putting things back in the wrong place, Tedesco proposed a walk over the hill to Woolford Mount. The only takers were Nicky and Barker.

"They are a huge credit to you, you know," he said as they set off down the lane.

"That's lovely of you, John, but Chag did play his part, especially when they were young. It wasn't me who taught them to swim, took them sailing, got Jack into rugby."

Once they had managed to negotiate the stile leading to the local beauty spot, Nicky found a suitable stick for Barker to retrieve.

"So, how is my brother-in-law?"

"Okay. Here goes. My lovely husband has decided that he is in love with Rochelle – yes, really, you couldn't make this, or her, up – and he has very kindly offered a clean-break divorce, but he wants the house to be sold and the proceeds split."

Tedesco, noticing Barker returning with the stick, took it off him and re-hurled it.

"Hmm. And you, understandably, want to stay put."

"It isn't that simple, but yes, I don't see why I should move out when he's the one with the mid-life crisis."

"So, and I can instantly feel myself regretting this, why isn't it simple?"

"He got me to sign some papers years ago. I'd forgotten about it until now. You are going to kill me because I just scrawled on them without your advice."

"Okay… so what have you done, Nicky? Signed the house over to him?"

"As good as. He has secured his business borrowings on Crane House, and I signed a consent form."

Tedesco took a sharp intake of breath. "And do you know how the business is going?"

After the walk, the rest of the evening was taken up with a riotous game of Monopoly. A new Rhyminster version had just been issued and so the family road-tested it, Uncle John being teased for the fact that properties in St Budeaux Place were on the cheap side, the Old Kent Road equivalent.

The game fizzled out once Jack had managed to build several hotels within the cathedral precincts – "You do realise that this would never be allowed," said his uncle – but as Tedesco had feared, the evening was not yet over for him as Nicky proposed a nightcap in the study.

Declining the offer of spirits – he had always studiously managed to avoid the top shelf of the drinks cabinet – he nevertheless greedily accepted another glass of Jos' claret.

"John, I know it's late but I'm really worried. What if the bank calls in Chag's loan?"

"The bank should have insisted that you received proper independent advice before you signed anything, so that would be the first point to look at. I don't suppose you remember if they did?"

"No, Chag basically told me to sign it – it was a 'mere technicality' is how he put it."

"Hmm, he did, did he? This could be significant. Look, why don't I mention this to one of my former partners? I'm seeing one of them tomorrow.

"Now, there's something I wanted to ask *you*. What did you make of our new bishop?"

FIVE

Having limited himself to the one glass in Nicky's study and having taken Barker for a decent walk through the village before breakfast, Tedesco was feeling in surprisingly good spirits the next morning as he headed back to Rhyminster to the nostalgic accompaniment of 'A World of Our Own' by the Seekers, which took him right back to his childhood in Plymouth.

Judith Durham, Mary Hopkin, Dusty Springfield, these had been the female voices of his formative years.

He was also looking forward to catching up with his old mate, and former partner in his law firm, Neil Sparkes.

Sparksy had become a recent convert to non-league football. "It's much more honest, John. No messing about with kick-off times, no overpaid prima donnas."

So, Tedesco had somewhat hesitantly agreed to go with Neil to see Rhyminster FC take on the might of Bridport in the Pengelly Pasties Western League.

He hadn't been to a game there for years, restricting his football watching to Plymouth Argyle, but was amused to see that Ken was still running the car park, the nice lady who sold the programmes was still there and the grumpy old guys he remembered from before were just as grumpy, just a bit older.

The stadium announcer hadn't changed either. "Come on, you Rebs, you Rebs, you Rebs – *aaaagh!*" he shouted as the home team took to the field.

For reasons that had been lost in the mists of time, Rhyminster were known as 'The Rebels'.

"You Rebs, you Rebs" sang what passed for the Rhyme Ultras.

"That announcer – he's a disgrace to the club," said one of the grumpy men, as he had repeated as a matter of ritual at every home match in living memory.

As the game got underway, Tedesco had forgotten quite how much time the ball spent in the air at this level, and how much energy was taken up in retrieving balls from the field behind the main stand. That said, he was enjoying it and the standard wasn't that bad.

After a goalless first half, in which the only real excitement had been when the Rebels had managed to gain a corner, the two former colleagues joined the queue at the refreshment hut.

"Two Bovrils, please," said Sparksy, knowing full well that Tedesco would approve. The decline in Bovril drinking at half time was yet another thing wrong with the modern world.

"As it's half time," said Tedesco, "I was wondering if you could recommend someone for some matrimonial work. It's for a friend."

Neil smiled. "It's for Nicky, isn't it? I was wondering when you'd ask. I know just the person to wipe the smile off that smug git Chag's face…"

As they made their way back to their seats, Tedesco heard the grumpy old men analyse what they had just seen.

"It wasn't bad for the first few minutes, but then it was back to normal. Misery and utter gloom."

"Yeah," said his partner in mirth. "A metaphor for life really."

As the second half wore on, the away team started to engage in blatant time wasting, or 'game management' as it is referred to these days, which meant the inevitable hail of abuse being directed at the poor referee both from the miserable old gits and from the Rhyminster manager, Brian Graddage, who was sent to the stands after one protest too many.

Tedesco was loving every moment.

Justice was done as the 'game management' plan failed spectacularly when the Rebs were awarded a penalty in time added on.

"I can't bear to watch" said Neil, as the kick was taken.

"*Goooaal*! You Rebs, you Rebs, you Rebs, *aaaagh*!" shouted the announcer.

"Why can't they sack that idiot? We know there's been a goal," said one of the miserable gits.

As if to make Tedesco's day, a group of outraged Bridport players surrounded the referee and, when the smoke had cleared, their captain was sent off. What a game!

He'd been enjoying watching the Rebs so much that he'd completely forgotten about Argyle.

"They lost. Three nil away to Rotherham," said Sparksy.

*

Sparksy, who had driven them to the out-of-town stadium, proposed a post-match pint in town so they could both walk home.

The Rhyminster Arms was just waking itself up before the serious night-time drinkers arrived. This was Tedesco's favourite time for a beer – early doors.

As they sipped their pints of Canon's Comfort, Neil broached the subject of Nicky's divorce.

"We have just recruited a promising lawyer from London – she's got a young family, the husband is in IT so he can work from home, so she's decided to join the exodus from the Smoke."

"And by so doing contributing to the housing crisis for our own young families."

"That was always your weak point as a lawyer – a social conscience. Any road, the terrifying Susannah Shaldon will be more than a match for whoever Chag instructs."

"Let me stop you there, Neil. Isn't collaborative law the thing now, seeking to reach a civilised end to a relationship rather than the aggressive approach you appear to be advocating?"

"Do you really think that your brother-in-law is the type to collaborate?"

Tedesco stroked his stubble. "Your round, I think."

SIX

Morning broke bright and clear, as if the heavens knew that it was Rhyminster's turn in the spotlight.

Tedesco had been up early after a busy dream-infested night and was to be found sitting outside in the garden drinking a pint of tea from his 'Green Army' mug, anticipating the day ahead with a combination of relish and foreboding.

Inaugurations of new Bishops of Rhyminster were rare events – Bishop James would only be the 79th, a tiny number given the 900-year history of the see.

He would be following in some giant footsteps, not least those of his immediate predecessor, as well as in those of some decidedly rum characters, such as the turncoat bishop who converted from Catholicism to Protestantism and back again and the Italian who spent all his days in Florence, never once visiting Rhyme.

Which camp would our new man fall into? Tedesco, pre-programmed to seek the very best in people, fervently hoped – and yes, prayed – that Bishop James would go with the grain of the gentle, but without being in any way weak, inclusive brand of Christianity that permeated the cathedral and its environs. But even he had to admit that the early signs were less than promising.

Within days of the announcement of his appointment, James Provan had held a number of 'one to one' meetings with what he referred to as 'key stakeholders', otherwise known to his predecessors as members of bishop's staff, his closest senior colleagues, and advisers.

Canon Wilf, the precentor, and the kindliest man under the sun, had uncharacteristically called round to 17 St Budeaux Place one evening without prior warning – he needed to let off steam.

Only an occasional drinker, he had on this occasion eagerly assisted his friend John in polishing off a bottle of Jos Elsted's own label St Emilion.

As Canon Wilfred explained, in the tactical absence of Dean Dan on a silent retreat, he had stood in for him as the cathedral's representative on the staff body.

"Bishop James wants us all to commit to studying for an MBA! How in the name of the Almighty is that going to help me do my job any better – or 'bleed into my role' as he so charmingly put it?"

The role of the canon precentor, whilst it did involve an element of people management, was primarily concerned with liturgy and music.

Tedesco nodded sympathetically, while Barker did his best to look concerned as Wilf's uncharacteristic rant gathered pace.

"Do you know what the archdeacon calls him? Spreadsheet Jim! He even referred to the 'C of E plc'!

"And – wait for this – we all must submit a business plan

for the diocese and the best one will go forward for further consideration! I have no idea what to do!"

"I know the best thing to do. Have another glass of pure velvet," said Tedesco, silently wondering whether the new bishop had added 'and at least one of you will be fired' to the explanation of his challenge.

He had been aware of other mutterings around the Close. The bishop's wife, an Australian academic called Stephanie Walker, had been making waves of her own.

Some of the Ladies of the Close had commented unfavourably on the retention of her maiden name – Tedesco was firmly with Ms Walker on this one – but she had also declined the kind offers of the Mother's Union, the Holy Dusters and the Guild of Flower Arrangers to be their patron.

Whilst allowing himself a wry smile when he heard the news, further reflection caused Tedesco to conclude that this had been a huge tactical blunder on the part of a newcomer.

It was the cathedral equivalent of alienating the Mafia, the Taliban and the KGB all at once. The special operations squad of the 'flower wrenchers' was not a group to cross lightly.

Tedesco's early morning musings were interrupted by the insistent beep of his new phone – an incoming text from his sister.

"Hi bro. I expect you've seen this morning's 'Times'. I'd love to know what you think. Oh – and I am seeing that lawyer your pal recommended."

As if on cue, Barker appeared at his side. "Oi, boss," he seemed to be saying, "isn't it part of the deal that you take me on a walk to the paper shop on Saturday mornings?"

If the local population had been aware of the significance of the events that were about to unfold at the cathedral, then they were making a good fist of concealing it.

Tedesco removed a copy of the *Times* from the display rack, then queued impatiently behind a hard-looking bloke in a high visibility tabard who was guzzling down a can of Red Bull, pausing only to ask for some Rizla papers and a ticket for EuroMillions.

How can the church ever connect with guys like that? the gentle detective thought.

His mood improved somewhat when he and his companion reached the front of the queue, where they were greeted by a smiling Agata. "Hi, John. And how are you today, Barker?" she said.

"I think it's going to be a long one," said Barker's expression.

Desperate to discover what Nicky had been alluding to in her text, he flew out of the little shop and leant against the river bridge, rifling excitedly through the list of features in his newspaper.

He found what he wanted in the main section – an exclusive interview with the new bishop under the headline 'How God sent me to cure England of Woke Christianity'.

SEVEN

Dean Dan's 'Very Reverend' WhatsApp group had sprung into action, as his fellow deans offered him heartfelt prayers of support.

The interview had included a section where Bishop James said that he would be ignoring the established convention whereby bishops did not interfere in the life of their cathedral. 'Two suspicious deaths amidst a culture of high living and complacency – there are obvious conclusions to be drawn.'

The new man had identified the choir as a prime target for his 'war on medieval flummery'.

Word of this had reached the Pelistry, the official residence of Charles Tantum the Master of Musick, who addressed his wife, Ginny, in his usual measured tones.

"Who in the name of Jerusalem the Sodding Golden does this ninny think he is?"

The new man had also indulged in some thinly veiled criticism of his predecessors: 'For too long, this diocese has typified the woke culture that has infested so many of our institutions. The "church militant" has become the "church hesitant", bowing to secular concepts of equality and gender fluidity at the expense of its core mission – the building of the kingdom in our own time, in strict accordance with scripture.'

Barker looked up with concern for his master as he read the article, steam almost literally coming from his ears.

Reading on, Tedesco learned that Bishop James blamed the pandering to liberal orthodoxy and the failure to condemn – a concept that had been disastrously allowed to go out of fashion – for both the decline in churchgoing and the concomitant tolerance of 'living in sin' and other 'alternative' lifestyles.

The interviewer later confessed herself to have been gobsmacked by the bishop's response to her final question.

"So, Bishop James, are you suggesting that the clock should be turned back to the fifties?"

"Now you tell me – why wouldn't that be a good start?"

"It's a bit early, Barker, but I could do with a glass of claret," said Tedesco, wondering how that afternoon's events would pan out. *Perhaps our new friend has got this off his chest in the press and he will be all sweet reason at the inauguration*, he thought, with little optimism.

*

It was as if the weather couldn't make its mind up about the new bishop either.

The sun was making brief, shy appearances before hiding behind the cloud cover, like a yawning teenager retreating back under the duvet.

Barker was given the afternoon off and so a solitary

Tedesco followed his familiar route out of St Budeaux Place and on into the Close via the South Gate.

The former diocesan registrar had been included on the list of cathedral worthies who were given reserved seats in the quire and he indulged himself in his usual feeling of pride and smugness as he waltzed through the packed main body of the cathedral. His mother would have been so proud. His internal jukebox clicked into place and selected Neil Sedaka: 'Standing on the Inside'.

The music that greeted him in the real world was by a somewhat different breed of singer-songwriter: César Franck, 'Cantabile'.

Then, with tedious inevitability, one of the sidesmen blocked his way before he could step up into the quire.

The Guild of Sidesmen now included women but this specimen shared an inherent officiousness with the more reactionary of the men.

Brandishing her clipboard as if it were an AK-47, she somehow managed the feat of simultaneously rolling her eyes to the heavens whilst addressing the man before her.

"Are you on my list?"

"I think you will find that I am."

"And who are you?"

Resisting the temptation to respond, Charles Tantum style, with 'Don't you know who I am you horrid little counter-jumper', he meekly introduced himself.

A queue built up as the official consulted her list, and, after finding the name Tedesco towards the end of the alphabet, which was hardly his fault, she admitted him into the holy of holies with a weary shrug and some more eye rolling.

Once he had located his place, he was delighted to find himself occupying a stall between the dean's wife and his friend Jos Elsted, the most discerning wine merchant in the south-west.

Jos was also a member of the Guild of Sidesmen, but he whispered to his friend that he had decided to avail himself of his reserved seat this time rather than volunteering for duty, a decision that had not gone down entirely well with some of his colleagues.

Silence descended as Dean Dan welcomed the congregation, drawn from across the diocese and beyond, featuring an impressive melange of foreign bishops from linked dioceses in Africa and Eastern Europe, as well as carnival processions of vergers, thurifers, residentiary canons, minor canons, lay canons, taperers and sundry other no doubt essential actors in the unfolding drama.

Jo, the dean's wife, whispered to Tedesco. "Medieval flummery alert."

"So, you read this morning's *Times* as well."

The dean wandered up to a microphone stand and then he confidently invited the congregation to stand and face the Great West Door, which had been wrenched open by two of the younger sidesmen to reveal the line-up of clergy and other dignitaries who had been marshalled by the head verger on the cathedral lawns.

Tedesco took a moment to reflect on how this scene would have been recognised by cathedral worshippers from across the centuries, his reverie shattered by the sight of a DPD delivery van being driven along the north walk.

The bishop was suddenly there, his great height causing him to need to stoop as he entered his cathedral where he was greeted in Latin by Charles Tantum, who was the nearest thing the cathedral had to a native speaker.

"Hodie discipuli," he roared, closing with a triumphant, "Salve, Episcope James!"

"I think we can safely say that the flummery warning lights are blazing red," whispered the former registrar, the resultant giggling from those in earshot being mercifully masked by the cathedral's famed Father Willis organ as it blasted out the opening bars of the first hymn, something modern by Graham Kendrick, who Tedesco would somewhat snootily refer to as the Ed Sheeran of church music.

In the aftermath of the service there would be much wailing and gnashing of dentures as the retired canons bemoaned the bishop's choice of music.

"It was liturgically rude, choosing stuff that no one knew..."

"Hear, hear. Bad start, Bishop James."

The service passed quickly. It was magnificent, the established church at its best. Yes, there were elements of pageantry and tradition that would not appeal to those of Bishop James' style of churchmanship, but, Tedesco felt, the ceremony was underscored by deep prayerfulness, inclusivity, and love.

He found himself moved beyond words as the new bishop made his formal oaths of allegiance, due obedience, and fidelity on the priceless Rhyme Bible, as well as feeling deeply reassured by the continuity of history.

After the final oath had been administered by the dean – in which the bishop swore to uphold the "Constitutions and Statutes, Ordinances and Laudable Customs of this Cathedral Church" – the ceremony moved on to the anointing and then the enthronement, after which the congregation, both physically present and watching via live-streaming, girded their loins for the bishop's first sermon.

EIGHT

The freshly minted, duly anointed and enthroned Bishop James climbed up the steps to the pulpit with a practised confidence.

Having reached the summit he took his time, surveying every inch of the cathedral.

Tedesco was reminded of school assemblies when he and his friends would quietly chant "Silence in the jungle, silence in the street, the world's biggest idiot is just about to speak", and then collapse with laughter when the headmaster spoke. He managed to control himself this time – he was a grown up now.

The bishop started promisingly enough, deploying comparatively modern cultural references to David Bowie and Sam Cooke to introduce his theme of change.

However, the changes that the 79th bishop was advocating were, as trailed, a direct challenge to modern orthodoxies.

"There will be some of you, maybe a majority, who would have revelled in what we have just witnessed," he said.

Cue polite Anglican shuffling in seats.

As Bishop James leaned out over the pulpit, Tedesco was put in mind of Orson Welles' cameo as the sermonising priest in *Moby Dick*.

"I have to tell you. I have to tell you the uncomfortable truth. What will any of this mean to those we seek to serve? Those to whom we have a mission. Those we need to convert."

Cue polite Anglican intakes of breath.

"I sense a discomfort in this building. I will repeat. Convert. This seems to have become a taboo, a dirty word. But I must level with you. If we don't increase our membership we will not only have failed in our historic mission but we will die. They will have won. The secularists. The liberals. The perverts, the sexually incontinent, those who prioritise political correctness over the word of scripture, the woolly-minded defeatists in our midst who are happy to preside over a steady decline. My message to you all is simple. A change is going to come. And I have been sent to make that change. So here is my challenge to the diocese. Join me in making the change or find something else to do. So, will you join me?"

As he descended from the pulpit the air was rent by a familiar sound, that of the Master of Musick.

"I fucking won't!"

An appalled Dean Dan looked on as the idiotic Charles made a point of exiting the quire and then walking the entire length of the nave, followed, to Tedesco's amazement, by Jos Elsted and a steady stream of other congregants.

The cathedral managed to pull itself together and get through the rest of the service, the dean somewhat rushing through the blessing as he realised with horror that there would be media gathering for the photographs and bun fight on the west lawn.

God seemed to have answered one of his most persistent prayers – to rid him of Tantum – but the Almighty was certainly moving in mysterious ways if this was the means.

There was an excited hum of conversation as the large congregation made its way out of the building under the watchful eyes of the sidesmen.

The sound was not unlike that of an excited theatre audience after a great performance, or a home football crowd exiting an old stadium like The Hawthorns or Fratton Park after a last-minute winner.

Normally after a major service like this the chatter would be about the music or the spectacle of the processions; this time, it was the bishop's sermon and the unprecedented response.

Tedesco reprised his 'hidden observer' thing, picking up a variety of reactions from "At least we are talking about the sermon for a change" to "Trust Charles to steal the show", and, more generally, variations on a theme of " What has the diocese done to deserve Bishop James?"

He fell into step with Lady Derrington, who was more diplomatic. "I think we should give the new chap a chance. He probably just wanted to make an impact."

"He's certainly done that. Shall I get us both a cup of tea?"

The cuppa that was provided was the bishop's choice – some kind of green, herbal concoction, which looked like one of those liquids that Z-list celebrities were forced to drink on a certain reality show. It tasted awful.

The detective and the bird-like aristocrat emerged onto the cathedral lawn and into bright sunlight. Tedesco joined the queue in the marquee while Lady Fiona went in search of her husband, Edward.

"Ah, John. Sanity at last!" It was the canon precentor.

"That's very kind of you, Wilf, but perhaps our new leader has a point? How will our kind of church survive?"

"Not by stigmatising minorities! Poor Jos, it must have taken courage to do what he did."

"Has anyone seen him?" said Tedesco, feeling a stab of anxiety for the kindly wine merchant.

Jos had settled into his life in the Cathedral Close after the untimely death of his civil partner and had discovered fellowship through his wine business, connecting with Bishop Bob, Dean Dan and Tedesco himself amongst many others.

He had become a sidesman and the Guild's ready acceptance of an openly gay man had cheered Tedesco's heart. He had allowed himself to think that the church – or at least Rhyminster Cathedral – really had become the welcoming, inclusive, safe place that it always should have been if it had been true to its founder.

Jos had also become an active street pastor, one of the brave souls who ministered to the night-time economy.

And now this new bishop had ruined all the good work.

Canon Wilf, having sensed that Tedesco needed a moment, took him gently by the arm. "Why don't you call Jos this evening, go and see him, or invite him over?"

"Thanks, Wilf. I think that's a splendid idea, as much for me as for Jos."

With that he left the marquee, found Lady Derrington and gave her the tea, accompanied by a warning that it might not be to her taste.

"I sense that we might be in need of something stronger I fear," she said, her elegant index finger indicating the sight of Charles Tantum being interviewed by Nicky Tedesco for BBC *Searchlight*.

NINE

Tedesco quietly slunk back to the refuge of 17 St Budeaux Place. Barker was clearly pleased to see him and so he wondered if an early evening walk was in order.

Perhaps Jos would like to come? He texted him, then nodded off on the sofa, eventually coming to with the realisation that it was Saturday afternoon and time for *Final Score*.

Argyle had drawn 1-1 away to Port Vale. He then googled the Pengelly Pasties League results: Rhyminster had managed the same result, away to Barnstaple.

All in all, not too bad. He resolved to contact Neil Sparkes to see if he fancied another trip to see 'The Rebs'.

"Woof!" said Barker. "Woof woof!"

"All right, old friend. It's only the phone."

The border terrier absolutely hated his master's Argyle anthem ring tone.

It was Jos. He sounded in need of company and was delighted to accept Tedesco's offer. Jos lived nearby in a small, but beautifully presented, flat on the far side of the Close, so he agreed to wander over in half an hour.

The early local news bulletin would be on soon, so Tedesco unmuted his smart TV and waited for the condescending national news reader to hand over for the "news wherever you are this evening".

Duncan Chivers had drawn the short straw and after running through the usual litany of traffic incidents and the local sport roundup, he handed over to Nicky outside the cathedral.

"There was unexpected drama at the inauguration of the new Bishop of Rhyminster today. After what some observers felt to have been a controversial sermon, the large congregation was stunned to witness a walk out led by the Director of Music, Charles Tantum, who joins me now."

"It is *Master* of Musick, a historic role which will be under threat if we take what was said today at face value," boomed Tantum.

Nicky was finding it hard to maintain BBC balance, but her innate professionalism won out.

"That is very interesting, Master. But is it true that you uttered an expletive in God's house? I am no expert, but I assume that will have consequences."

"We all have limits to our tolerance, Ms Tedesco. And if I am going to be the last holder of my ancient office I am not going down without a fight."

Nicky looked straight down the barrel of the camera.

"So, as the cathedral tries to recover from the still recent murders and deaths, there is no sign of any respite from the dramas that continue to beset this iconic building. This is Nicola Tedesco, for BBC *Searchlight*."

After listening to Duncan Chivers announcing that a fuller report would feature on Monday's *Searchlight Tonight*

– which Tedesco affectionately referred to as 'Cat Stranded up Tree' – the detective angrily zapped the remote. He would call Nicky tomorrow...

*

An eager terrier greeted Jos Elsted at the door, his reaction to his new friend being how you imagined your favourite Irish granny would feel if she was about to be introduced to Daniel O'Donnell.

Barker hadn't really met Jos, but his innate canine radar instantly registered the wine merchant as dog friendly.

"Hello, Barker!" said Jos, with real warmth, reaching down to stroke him.

"I'm really looking forward to our little outing. I wonder where John is taking us?"

"Jos! Welcome to life outside the Close! I thought we could have a stroll around Creber Lake as its still light enough and then back here for a takeaway?"

"Sounds good to me – and Barker clearly agrees."

The little dog was wagging his tail at record speed.

Barker jumped into the rear of the Lancia while Jos sat in the front passenger seat.

The conversation was light while they drove to the lake, an old reservoir that had been developed as a relaxed space for walking and some gentle water sports.

Jos hadn't been there before and was transfixed. "This is wonderful, John. I really need to explore the local area more. Since moving down from London, I have tended to stay in Rhyme."

"Nothing wrong with that. I can tell that you love the

place, and that it loves you," said Tedesco, wondering where that came from – it wasn't his usual cautious lawyerly use of words.

"That's why I was so angry, John. It took a while to settle in a new city without my soulmate, but recently I have come to think of Rhyme as my first real home, where I am accepted for who I am, where I have lovely customers like you and where…"

"Go on," said Tedesco, gently.

"God, aren't we Anglicans hopeless when it comes to discussing faith? Okay, where I found belief, almost despite myself."

Barker looked up expectantly, so Tedesco produced a tennis ball from his barn jacket and hurled it just inside the lake. The border terrier was an excellent swimmer.

Jos continued with more confidence. "It wasn't a blinding flash or being born again. I still find that stuff a bit pseudo – it was gradual."

Tedesco's internal playlist: Dylan, *Slow Train*.

He welcomed Barker back from his icy dip, then responded to Jos.

The detective also found it hard to discuss faith, but in the spirit of openness he asked Jos if his experience had been like his own: the result of spending time with good, practical, people who happened to be Christians. After a while he realised that there must be something in it if Canon Wilf and Bishop Bob, two of the most sane, rational beings he knew, had faith. It seemed to give them an extra dimension. It impressed Tedesco because it wasn't showy or demonstrative. Neither of them had openly tried to convert him or bring him to God. But their example of the good life was one he tried to follow.

The two friends walked around the lake in companionable silence, stopping every now and then to entertain Barker with the tennis ball.

"That's why I felt so cross, and worried about the future. If Bishop James is right then I'm no longer welcome in the church – he sees people like me as unnatural, deviant."

Tedesco smiled at his friend. It always amused him to see how Jos had adopted a uniform since his move from London. He always wore a check shirt with a woollen gilet, which for some reason reminded him of Paddington Bear.

"You will always be welcome at the cathedral – look how many followed you. What you did was brave and principled, not like Charles and his self-indulgent stunt."

"I feel that I've let the dean down…"

"Stop right there. If I know Dan, he would have been with you all the way, although he could never admit it in public. Look, if you are worried why don't you make an appointment to see him? I think you both need support. You agree, don't you, Barker?"

TEN

It would be good to be able to report that the atmosphere in Rhyminster and the surrounding diocese had stabilised after the explosive start to the bishop's term of office.

With no little sadness it has to be revealed that the following weeks and months bore witness to a litany of dramas and scandals worthy of the last days of Boris Johnson.

Here are some selected highlights:

Bishop James appointed Keith Neighbour, an old colleague from the Diocese of Sydney, as his lay assistant. It soon became clear that the self-declared 'Neighbour from Hell' was put there to undermine Amanda, the diocesan secretary.

Ms Leonard, who oozed capability from every pore, soon found herself placed in an impossible position and so she resigned. She was swiftly headhunted into a new post as Chief Executive of the Solicitors Regulatory Authority. She is suing the diocese for constructive dismissal. The diocese is seeking leave to introduce the bishop as a third party in the litigation.

Keith Neighbour immediately accepted the newly created position of Chief of Staff, or Chief Executive. He was rumoured to enjoy a six-figure salary with a bonus scheme based on increasing congregations. His salary was reputed to be covered by anonymous evangelical groups in the USA.

The diocesan clergy, with the possible exception of the most extreme evangelicals, were up in arms. Not only had the Neighbour from Hell imposed ambitious recruitment targets for new worshippers, but either he or one of his energetic team of 'soul seekers' would bombard the poor clerics with motivational texts and messages – "Rev. Chris, how many new members have you achieved this week? Go big, Chris!"

A digital resources hub had been developed, so that parishes could access a bespoke toolkit to help them reach their externally set goals. As one churchwarden commented, a real toolkit and someone who could fix the boiler might be more use.

Bishop James introduced standard sermons, written, or 'curated' by the great man himself, which the benighted clergy had to read out instead of writing their own.

These sermons had to be delivered at the exact same time in every parish church, both in person and via video link.

The bishop, aided by his new chief of staff, had developed a huge media profile. As well as his own social media channels he had effectively hi-jacked those of the diocese and the individual parishes, which contributed to a growing cult of personality.

He became a regular on *Question Time* and *Any Questions*, as well as having syndicated columns in the local press. The *Daily Mail* featured a glowing leading article describing him as 'God's Tory'.

After the bishop refused the offer to join LGBT+ Christians at Rhyme Pride – an event that was a highlight of

Bishop Bob's year – Jos Elsted was joined by various notables including the dean's wife Jo, Lady Derrington and Tedesco and Lynne Davey in a silent vigil outside the North Canonry.

But surely, at least the cathedral itself could remain above the fray, a refuge from the zealots and the bishop's growing personality cult?

Up to a point, Lord Copper.

Whilst the dean was immune from the compulsory sermons – any attempt to interfere with his independence would result in Keith Neighbour being firmly reminded of the bishop's solemn declaration to uphold the constitution and customs of the cathedral – the bishop retaliated by studiously staying away, even going to the length of conducting ordination services in sports halls.

At the same time, Neighbour ran an effective spin campaign against the cathedral, trying to drive a wedge between cathedral and diocese, bishop and dean. The dean and chapter was branded as the 'cultural elite' who despised modern worship, preferring to be stuck in a medieval time warp. The bishop, of course, was on the side of 'real people', the battlers and the strivers.

Charles Tantum was still in post, although suspended on full pay awaiting the result of a hastily commissioned external enquiry.

Tedesco, observing from his privileged position of slight detachment, felt that all this couldn't go on without some kind of explosion. The centre simply couldn't hold.

The dean was clearly of similar mind, so Tedesco found himself one of a select group who were invited to meet at a retreat centre just outside the diocese in Somerset. It was called, with grim irony, 'The Safe House'.

The invitation, hand-delivered in the early hours of the morning, contained an injunction not to disclose the matter to anyone else. However, Tedesco's letter included a handwritten postscript.

'Border terriers will be very welcome.'

ELEVEN

So, it was with a mixture of excitement and sheer trepidation that Tedesco and Barker climbed into the Lancia and set off for Somerset in the early hours of the appointed Saturday morning.

Relieved that he lived just outside the Close, otherwise he would have needed to wrestle with the key to unlock the South Gate at that ridiculous hour, and pleased to see that Barker was soon asleep again, he used the vanity light to check the directions – he pointedly didn't own a sat nav – and then he followed the signs towards Exeter.

He'd already selected some suitable music – Van Morrison, *Inarticulate Speech of the Heart*, which was just right for the early hour and the direction: towards mythical Avalon.

He kept going until Taunton Deane services where he and Barker enjoyed what his brother-in-law would charmingly refer to as a 'Penelope Piss-Stop', followed by a black coffee to keep him awake for what remained of his journey.

It was just getting light as they reached the outskirts of Frome, where the detective lost his bearings before being directed to Mells by a most helpful woman taking her Jack Russell for an early morning walk.

He thanked her profusely. "That's all right. Have a good day, my lovely," she replied.

The Safe House was located beyond the small but perfectly formed village of Mells. Driving through, he noticed the tower of the huge parish church, remembering that Siegfried Sassoon was buried in the graveyard and resolving to call in on his return journey.

He checked his watch – breakfast would be served from eight, so he was bang on time.

The venue for the secretive gathering was at the end of a large, overgrown drive; Tedesco wondered if assassins in black polo necks were patrolling the grounds, like in a black and white episode of *The Avengers*.

As he hadn't been allowed to advise Lynne of his location, she wouldn't be able to rescue him, Emma Peel style, if he found that he'd been lured into a trap.

He needn't have fretted – parking outside the somewhat grim, pebble-dashed front of the building he saw the reassuring sight of Lady Derrington's Mini Clubman.

"Don't worry, Barker, we are among friends."

His mood was further lifted when the door was opened by Barbara Battershill, secretary to the last three bishops of Rhyminster. She had had the good sense to retire with Bob and so had avoided any dealings with Jim Il Sung or the Neighbour from Hell, not that either of them would have fazed her.

Her eyes lit up at the sight of Barker, who she bent down and stroked.

Getting back to her feet, she greeted Tedesco.

"I'm not surprised to see you here – it looks as if the dean has rounded up the A team!"

Barbara ushered Tedesco into a vast kitchen, which was hosting a sumptuous buffet breakfast, and then she led Barker off for some unspecified admin tasks.

Dean Dan stood up and greeted him. "Well done, John. Sorry about the cloak and dagger stuff, but you will soon find out why. Can I get you some coffee? Help yourself to some breakfast – the sausages are delicious."

Tedesco was ravenous and stacked his plate with various pork products – sausage, black pudding, and back bacon – as well as some token vegetables, albeit of the fried variety.

Sitting next to Dan, he learned that the retreat house was a private initiative run by a non-stipendiary clergy couple who owned the farm next door. They had converted two adjoining farm workers' cottages to form the Safe House, and they employed some 'ladies from the village' to do the catering.

Ronnie was a gentleman farmer and Maddie worked in the city, returning at weekends.

Although they both ministered part-time in the diocese of Bath and Wells, they had become so concerned about events in Rhyminster diocese that they had offered free use of the facilities for the day.

The other delegates soon arrived. As well as Lady Fiona, Tedesco spotted Sir Vere Alston, the former MP for Rhyminster, and, to his delight, his friend the precentor, Canon Wilfred Drake.

There were two others, one he vaguely recognised and one he didn't, a languid-looking woman who looked like a pre-Raphaelite portrait come to life. She probably owned an art gallery in Frome or Bruton.

As the breakfast plates were about to be cleared away, the dean got to his feet and explained that the meeting would start in ten minutes in the conference room, which was to be found in an extension at the far end of the building.

"All will be revealed!"

*

Dan commenced with a prayer, asking for God's blessing on the important matters that the group would be discussing and for wisdom in coming to any conclusion about how to move forward together.

The meeting would be facilitated by Dr Ruth Warwick, Archdeacon of the Isle of Wight – the languid lady who had caught Tedesco's eye – and Barbara Battershill would be taking the minutes. Barker, sitting attentively near the front, was announced as the group's wellness champion and therapy dog.

The members of the group were then identified in turn.

"We have John Tedesco, our former diocesan registrar, Canon Wilf Drake of course, Lady Derrington—"

"Do call me Fiona."

"—Sir Vere Alston and, representing the parish clergy, Henry Easton, rector of Derrington with Hillbrook and the driving force behind the Street Pastors."

Ah, that's who he is, thought Tedesco. He'd seen him talking to Lady Fiona at various events and Jos had spoken highly of him in the context of the Street Pastors.

"Wilf and I have called this meeting because our inboxes have been crammed with questions about the new regime from throughout the diocese and beyond," said the dean.

The precentor then took over. "Many of our diocesan clergy have been quizzed by their regular worshippers about the quality of the sermons – several people have commented that they are more like party political broadcasts – and Dan and I have been given discreet messages of support from other dioceses. The Dean of Salisbury told me that he felt that Rhyminster was becoming like Russia and is worried that Bishop James might have expansionary plans."

At this point, Dean Dan asked Ruth Warwick to facilitate the discussions.

"Thank you, Dan. You have all been chosen for your expertise and experience in church affairs and with particular reference to the life of your historic diocese. This will be an open forum and, although Barbara will be taking notes, any transcripts will be sent only to those of us present and they will be fully encrypted and password protected. I hope you will all feel free to speak frankly."

Tedesco noticed Barker stretching – perhaps he could be used to sweep the room for any suspicious listening devices?

He was snapped back to attention by Dr Warwick.

"John. Let's start with you. As the former legal adviser to the diocese, what concerns do you have?"

Tedesco took a moment to order his thoughts.

"First of all, I am concerned for the financial viability of the diocese. Even if Jim Il Sung succeeds in converting every living soul in the place, there could be a tsunami of litigation coming our way."

"How so?" said Dr Ruth.

"Where to begin! The Neighbour from Hell is exposing the diocese to countless potential claims of bullying. If the bishop carries out his threats to fire any clergy who fail to meet his recruitment targets, then there will be unfair dismissal claims, or expensive compromise agreements. The new regime's attitude to minorities could bring us into conflict with anti-discrimination laws – what an awful thing to have to articulate."

He paused for breath. "Neither Bishop James nor Keith Neighbour seem to pay any attention to ecclesiastical law. It seems to me that the bishop is breaking solemn vows to only use the forms of service as laid down by canon, and his 'Lord Sugar' approach to firing clergy completely ignores the fact that some of them still have freehold. And then there is the question of reputational damage."

"Thank you, John. We may return to the image problem later. Now, Lady Fiona. You are on Bishop's Council and your husband is the patron of several parishes. What has been your experience of the 79th bishop?"

TWELVE

Barker, sensing Her Ladyship's anxiety, had parked himself beside her, so Lady Fiona was able to give him a stroke before she began to speak.

"You said we should be frank. I have never been spoken to so rudely in my life. Mr Neighbour came to our parochial church council last month and told us that we were an embarrassment as there was no one present under the age of sixty years old. When our darling churchwardens tried to explain how hard it was to keep the building maintained for future generations, this awful man said, 'Not my problem, mate,' or words to that effect. And I have heard the same from the other villages. He even referred to Aubrey Crocker over at Woolford as a dinosaur!"

Dr Ruth, correctly sensing a lengthy rant, thanked the bird-like aristocrat for her contribution and then asked Henry Easton to speak.

"Henry, I know that you interact with a lot of people, including the young. What changes have you noticed?"

Henry Easton was a bachelor in late middle age who had become ordained after a career as a naval officer. He was the type of chap that Tedesco's mother would have described as having a kind face.

"Let me start with a positive comment. The new forms of worship are going down well in some of our suburban parishes, and there is evidence to show that this is increasing interest amongst the younger generations. But it is patchy, and the positivity is outweighed by the unwelcoming stance when it comes to the LGBT+ community, to which John alluded earlier."

"Do you have any specific examples?"

"Apart from Bishop James first sermon, which led to a walk out, you mean? And his refusal to attend or even offer a message of support to Pride?"

Barker trotted over to Henry, who cuddled him before continuing.

"Sorry, I get a little heated over this. It isn't so much a question of instances of explicit homophobic or transphobic comments, it's the cultural shift. We must ask ourselves: what kind of church are we if great people like Jos Elsted no longer feel welcome?"

"Hear hear," said Canon Wilf, adding that at least the cathedral was rapidly becoming a safe haven for lovers of traditional worship as well as for minorities and independent thinkers.

Sir Vere Alston cleared his throat.

"It pains me to say that my experience mirrors that of the rest of you. And John Tedesco is right: the reputation not just of our wonderful diocese – for so long the envy of others – but of the entire church is being compromised. Is there nothing we can do to stop this before it's too late?"

Ruth Warwick looked up. "I think you have all made

some useful initial points, and to sum up, the general view is that something needs to be done. As John will no doubt confirm, it is practically impossible to remove a bishop from office. So, is there any prospect of persuading him to be more open, more willing to hear other views? Perhaps we could ponder this over tea and coffee? Let's reconvene in fifteen minutes."

Tedesco collected a mug of coffee from the kitchen and then took Barker into the garden. The border terrier needed a comfort break as well as a quick woof and sniff in his temporary surroundings.

As Barker eagerly chased the tennis ball, Dr Ruth joined Tedesco.

"Barker has certainly fulfilled his brief – I saw the way he calmed down Lady Fiona and Henry. You must be very proud of him."

"Oh, I very much am," said the former legal adviser as Barker dropped the ball at his feet.

"We all love Barker," said Lady Fiona, arriving with Sir Vere.

THIRTEEN

Bishop James was an early riser. After a workout on his rowing machine, he took the pace down with a jog around the Close before anyone else was moving. Once he had showered, he retreated to his cell-like study to pray.

He had an exciting day ahead of him. He was the keynote preacher at the 'Soaked by the Spirit' festival in Somerset. It was events like this that really motivated him.

He prayed for the Lord to use his gifts of communication as a channel to bring more lost souls to Christ, and to help the forces of reaction in the cathedral and the diocese to repent of their sins and support his historic mission, before joining his wife, Stephanie, for a simple breakfast of granola and yogurt, washed down with green herbal tea, the only stimulant to pass his lips. This was the same noxious brew that he had insisted upon offering at the bunfight after his inauguration.

As many in the Close had noted, the North Canonry had ceased to be the welcoming place that it had been throughout its recent history. It was now used solely as a place of work, and so there had been no invitations issued to the likes of

Tedesco to come round to sample Elsted's wine – indeed, not a drop of wine had been sipped in the building, other than as part of holy communion, since the arrival of the 79th bishop.

Little had been seen of Stephanie Walker in Rhyminster, as she was a Professor of Christian Economics at Bristol University and lived there during the week.

Tedesco had asked Lynne to carry out some background checks on 'Mrs Bishop', which revealed that she owned a flat in the affluent Clifton area, where she spent her weeks. Ms Walker was the daughter of 'Ocker' Walker, a media mogul who, while not in the league of Rupert Murdoch or the fictional Logan Roy, was still a significant player in the Pacific Rim. She was rumoured to have used some of her father's spare cash to bankroll her husband's missionary work.

Over breakfast, the bishop and his wife discussed their forthcoming day ahead, Stephanie relishing the chance to get down to work on her forthcoming series of essays entitled 'Ayn Rand: lessons for the modern Christian'.

As they were clearing away dirty crockery, the security gates – another innovation of the new regime – swung open, allowing Keith Neighbour's Range Rover through.

"Have a productive time," said Stephanie as the bishop went to join his chief of staff, chauffeur, and henchman.

*

As Jim Il Sung and the Neighbour from Hell headed away from the Close, the Escape Committee was reconvening after their coffee break.

Dr Ruth welcomed them back. "So, let's have some

suggestions. How can we heal the divisions? Canon Wilf, what can you tell us?"

"Apart from asking who will rid us of this turbulent bishop, do you mean? He doesn't seem to want to listen to anyone, so all I can suggest is that the dean gives tacit approval for our clergy to go back to writing their own sermons, using the prayer book if that's what their congregation is used to, and see if Jim gets the message."

"We could boycott Keith Neighbour's ridiculous away days for clergy. Did you hear about the last one? It was led by an army sergeant major, who got us all in a boxing ring and told us to start fighting each other and then yelled at us when we wouldn't," said Henry Easton.

Sir Vere, a man of few, but decisive, words gave his opinion.

"I regret to say that we may have to seek advice about removing him. There is a precedent of sorts, not a million miles away. I think we need a legal view – John?"

"What Sir Vere is alluding to, as I expect you all know, is what happened in the diocese of Kirkminster a decade or so ago. They suffered from an egotistical bishop who was threatening to bankrupt the diocese."

"I think I remember," said Lady Fiona, "and didn't they pass a vote of no confidence or something?"

"They had tabled such a motion for diocesan synod," Tedesco answered, "but the efficacy and legality of this was never tested as Bishop Harray stood down before the synod could meet, on the grounds of ill health."

"So could we test this now?" asked Dean Dan.

Tedesco gave Barker a stroke, and then responded. "I think I need to do some research and prepare a briefing paper. The then registrar at Kirkminster has retired like me, but I can get hold of him and pick his brains."

"We will need to get some senior members of bishop's staff on board," said Lady Fiona, Wilf Drake adding that they would need to be pretty certain of the likely response from the individuals in question before any approach was made.

It was left that Tedesco would look into the feasibility of a vote of no confidence and report back, while the other members would take informal soundings from folk around the diocese.

However, by the time that Tedesco and Barker had arrived back at St Budeaux Place, having stopped off at Mells to see Sassoon's memorial, the need for his research would have disappeared.

FOURTEEN

"What a long day, old friend," said Tedesco as he let Barker out of the Lancia.

He'd been listening to *Sports Report* as they got closer to home. Argyle had beaten Fleetwood Town at Home Park, so he was in a good mood, looking forward to a quiet night in.

No chance. As he entered the house, he saw that the answering machine on the landline was flashing red. He'd turned his mobile phone off when driving, and as soon as he switched it back on again the Argyle ring tone blared with an almost aggressive intensity.

"Nicky! Are you okay? Have you seen the solicitor yet?"

"No, look, I wanted to see how you were?"

This puzzled the ex-lawyer. "I'm okay, medium rare – look, sis, you can tell me, you know?"

"Derr! It's about the bishop! Haven't you heard?"

"Heard what?"

"I don't believe this! Where have you been all day? Bishop James was found dead at some happy-clappy rally. It's been all over the news. Have you been to the Close yet?"

"No. I suppose there will be reporters. Good God! His poor wife! Do we know what happened?"

"The police are being tight-lipped, but the rumour mill has it that he was stabbed in the back – literally."

After closing the call, Tedesco filled Barker's bowl, poured himself a large glass of claret, and played back his messages. They were all about the late bishop.

The TV news would be on soon, so in the meantime he tried to order his thoughts by selecting a suitable track, settling on vintage Clifford T Ward: 'Crisis'.

Over at the festival the organisers had been in two minds. Do they send everyone home – which could be a logistical nightmare – or do they carry on regardless, as the bishop might have wanted?

The Avon and Somerset constabulary made the decision for them, declaring the entire site a crime scene, and after issuing a plea for witnesses they supervised an orderly evacuation.

The news soon spread to the diocese of Rhyminster, which found itself once again without a bishop. Pete Leiper, the Bishop of Dartmoor, who had been in charge during the interregnum, prepared to stand in again.

Back at Tedesco's bolthole, the retired registrar caught up with his messages, including an urgent summons from Dean Dan, and then he switched on the TV.

There were no details of how the 79th bishop had met his end, but the implications were clear: the police had not ruled out foul play.

The local *Searchlight* bulletin featured Duncan Chivers reporting from outside the cathedral. *Poor sod must have hot-footed it from Argyle, probably missed most of the second half,* was Tedesco's first, somewhat cynical thought, the second being what Julie Stringer, the indefatigable reporter from the *Rhyminster Journal* would be up to.

Then he sprang into action, texting Lynne, explaining to a confused Barker that he would be on his own for a while, before heading out through the Close, then across the Green to the deanery.

He needn't have bothered texting his colleague – her bike was chained to the deanery wall.

FIFTEEN

Jo Luxmoore, the dean's wife, and part-time PA, led Tedesco into the study, where he found Sir Vere Alston, Bishop Pete, Canon Wilfred and the dean himself, as well as Lynne.

"John, welcome. I was explaining to the others that I called in as many of you as I could get hold of at short notice, as much to help me try and get a handle on what had just happened as anything else. Lady Fiona is staying up in Somerset with some friends, so sends her apologies and is thinking of us all. We have just said a prayer for James and his poor family. And Henry Easton is where he always is on Saturday nights, ministering to the night-time economy."

The Bishop of Dartmoor, Pete Leiper, leapt in.

"Sorry to interrupt, Dan, but before we go much further, I think it is right for me to let the meeting know that you have filled me in about the gathering at the Safe House earlier, so there's no need to tiptoe around this."

"Pete, I'm grateful," said the dean, who then turned to Tedesco and Davey.

"John, perhaps you could bring Lynne up to speed about this morning later, but the reason I've brought you both in is that I think your input could be invaluable over the current weeks."

Sir Vere Alston, correctly sensing that Dan was cuing him in, added: "We are in unchartered waters – the media are already speculating that this could be the first time that an English bishop has been murdered since Thomas à Becket, and the legal position of the diocese is somewhat uncertain."

Canon Wilf explained that although the bishop had died outside the diocese, and that the matter was in the hands of a neighbouring force, the late James Provan was very much a Rhyminster problem, and therefore it seemed inconceivable that the Devon and Cornwall constabulary wouldn't be taking an interest in proceedings.

At this point a disconcerted Lynne found herself drifting off into an inner soundtrack of her own: Robin Thicke, 'Blurred Lines'.

While she reflected with some concern how overexposure to her colleague could be interfering with her cognitive functions – literally doing her head in – Tedesco was tuning into his defiantly late 20th century jukebox: Billy Joel, 'Shades of Grey'.

Lynne was the first to snap out of it.

"Dan, I know I'm late to the party on this, but John retired years ago. Can't his successor advise the diocese?"

The ginger-haired local boy made good, Pete Leiper, who resembled what Josh Widdicombe might have looked like if he'd become a bishop instead of a comedian, spoke up.

"I'll take this one. You are quite right, Lynne, we do have a diocesan registrar, the second one since John retired. But as David has only been in post for a matter of a few months, and while he and the chancellor will of course have to advise me on legal matters in this sudden interregnum, John is in a unique position."

Sir Vere leant in towards Lynne. "You see, no one knows the politics of the diocese like John, and he has the additional super-power – as my grandson would say – of his detective skills. I am sure I speak for us all in saying that I don't know how we would have managed without you both during the turmoil of the last few years."

"I hope you are including Barker in this paean of praise," added Canon Wilf, provoking some welcome smiles from around the room.

Tedesco removed his glasses for theatrical effect.

"So, if I understand things correctly, you want Lynne and I to keep our ears to the ground as matters develop."

Canon Wilf had been staring at his phone, with an increasingly worried expression.

"There are already unconfirmed reports from the scene that suggest that Bishop James was stabbed. I'm beginning to regret my little joke about ridding us of this turbulent bishop…"

The dean stood up to signal that business was over.

"If there is anything in this, then we will indeed need our best detectives on the case. Jo and I are going over to see Stephanie. I only hope that these rumours haven't reached her yet."

As the little gathering broke up, the security gates at the North Canonry swung open and Keith Neighbour drove through.

SIXTEEN

Time for a little catch-up on the weeks following the sensational happenings at 'Soaked by the Spirit':

The police confirmed that the bishop had been killed by a single, violent knife attack.

The place of death was at Charters Farm, the festival venue. The bishop had apparently been attacked in a yurt, which operated as a changing area cum green room for VIP guests, just as he was composing himself before taking to the stage.

There was no CCTV in the yurt, but several eyewitnesses had mentioned a helmeted figure on a motorbike speeding away from the festival site while the worship band was playing.

Keith Neighbour, who would have been expected to have been with the bishop at all times, was instead captured on film with his arms aloft in the 'Celestial Mosh Pit' around the time that his employer met his end.

Pressure was growing on the church authorities to speed up the process for the appointment of a new bishop, with a growing campaign to make Pete Leiper's appointment a permanent one.

Stephanie Walker had moved out of the North Canonry, but Keith Neighbour kept an office there and continued to administer the diocese.

Nicky Tedesco had instructed her solicitor to issue divorce proceedings.

What hadn't been made public was the peculiar image found on the bishop's back when one of the security team discovered his dead body.

At first blush, it had appeared as if a large letter 'A', like something out of a medieval manuscript, had painstakingly been carved into the body.

It soon transpired that the 'carving' had been inked on, and having established with an exasperated bishop's wife that her husband had no tattoos – "Are you seriously suggesting…" – the issue was foxing the investigating officers, led by DCI Verena Hill of the Avon and Somerset force.

DCI Hill was a contemporary of DCI Jimmy Bloomfield, Rhyminster's senior officer, and so she decided to get in touch with him, as if anyone 'got' Rhyme and the politics of church and diocese, Bloomfield did, albeit through the conduit of the small detective agency in Minster Precincts.

"Jimmy – you will guess what this is about. We still aren't getting anywhere quickly and there is an aspect that is defeating us. We need someone who understands church stuff on this, and I was thinking…"

"Let me stop you there. It's not me you need, it's Tedesco and Davey."

*

Meanwhile, the two detectives had been keeping an eye on developments, as they had been asked to do by Dean Dan and the Escape Committee.

Lynne had been looking into the backgrounds of the bishop, the Neighbour from Hell and Stephanie Walker. She had unearthed some interesting stuff, which even drew a semi flamboyant "*molto interessante*" from her habitually restrained colleague.

Neighbour, after a spell serving in the Australian marines, had risen to become a high-ranking executive in Stephanie's father's media conglomerate, the Larrikin Group.

His last job was running the religious broadcasting arm, which was about as far removed from *Songs of Praise* as Angela Rayner was from membership of the 1922 Committee of backbench Tory MPs.

Neighbour's role was to promote right-wing Christian evangelism both through legacy media and the Larrikin Group's extensive streaming services and platforms.

Stephanie's father, Ocker, had correctly identified the synergy between Sydney diocese style churchmanship and blue-collar politics, the rise of which could only benefit his empire.

Of more prurient interest, Lynne had seen several photos featuring the now bishop's wife and the Neighbour from Hell in which the two of them seemed, shall we say, quite friendly...

"Perhaps that's when good neighbours become good friends, Lynne," said Tedesco, which was met with eye rolling followed by a groan.

"Seriously though," he went on, "if Stephanie and Neighbour knew each other from way back, and they met through her father, then this whole thing becomes quite sinister, doesn't it?"

Lynne shrugged her shoulders. "Sorry, John, you are going weird on me. I have literally no idea what you are on about."

"Fair point. Let me explain."

She cut him short. "Mansplain, you mean."

"Mrs Davey, you have cut my new man heart into ten thousand pieces. Let me *share* with you. Better?"

"Nice try. Pray continue."

"Okay. So, old man Walker has a political agenda, which is to keep mogul-friendly governments in power. He has had, I think you will agree, considerable success down under in linking the Christian Right with anti-woke politics to keep taxes low and climate as far down the agenda as possible.

"Then his brilliant daughter hooks up with a future bishop of the Church of England and old Ocker senses a chance to repeat the trick over here."

"I think I see where you are going. He gives Stephanie the splendid idea of luring Keith Neighbour over here, sorts out a salary package way in advance of what the diocese could pay."

"Stephanie persuades Bishop James that Neighbour is the answer to his prayers. Amanda Leonard wakes up and smells the coffee, leaving a clear opening."

"And the dear old Church of England that we know and love becomes part of the terrifyingly certain world of the mega church future."

Lynne put her feet up on Tedesco's desk, which he always found disconcerting.

"And someone out there felt sufficiently threatened to murder a bishop."

SEVENTEEN

Sally Munks, the agency's loyal but occasionally infuriating PA, put the call through to Tedesco, offering him her unsolicited opinion that it sounded important.

"Tedesco speaking. How can I help?"

It was DCI Verena Hill from Avon and Somerset police.

"I hope you don't mind me calling, but DCI Bloomfield has suggested that you might be able to help us on a certain matter. You came highly recommended."

Tedesco resisted the temptation to say, 'I've been expecting you, Ms Bond', instead opting for a sense of slight bewilderment.

"Well, that's very good of Jimmy, but this all sounds rather conspiratorial to my simple mind. Could we meet somewhere neutral? And I would want my colleague Lynne to be there."

"Of course. Could I suggest your offices, say 6pm tomorrow?"

They must be desperate, he thought, knowing full well what it was about as Bloomfield had already given him the heads up.

Lynne, however, was less than gruntled as this would mean a late appearance at her yoga class – again.

"Oh well, Jo is getting used to me letting her down, I suppose. Have you seen the *Journal*?"

The *Rhyminster Journal*, a rare survivor in the endangered species that was local papers, was not Tedesco's normal reading of choice.

"Okay, what's Julie written about this time?"

Julie Stringer had been entertaining the *Journal*'s ageing readership for more years than she would like to admit with her weekly 'It Makes Me Mad' column.

"Take a look."

Lynne had folded the newspaper to reveal Julie's column, which customarily featured a somewhat flattering picture of a much younger Julie angrily ripping up what appeared to be utility bills.

The target for the veteran reporter's synthetic rage this week was the lack of progress in the police investigation.

"'So, this week,'" Tedesco read aloud, "'I've interviewed the only person who seems to care about the murder of our bishop, the lovely Keith Neighbour.'"

He stood up and looked out over the medieval rooftops of Rhyme.

"Keith Neighbour! Lovely? Really?"

"I expect she fancies him. And he is, as the youngsters say, quite hench. A complete bastard, but a complete bastard who quite clearly works out."

Reading on, they gleaned that the Chief Executive of the Diocese was continuing in the job out of a sense of duty, nothing mentioned about his six-figure salary.

Tedesco had been consulted by Pete Leiper and the current

diocesan registrar about ways of terminating Neighbour's contract, but it seemed that there was nothing that could be done until a permanent appointment of a new bishop had been made, unless Keith was found guilty of gross misconduct.

Neighbour had convinced Julie – not widely known for her gullibility unless she was in the presence of an attractive younger man with a pulse – that he was single-handedly keeping the diocese afloat while Pete Leiper, the dean and the other church worthies did nothing, and also that the police seemed to have given up on their investigation.

*

Having shooed Sally safely off the premises, Lynne tidied the agency's little conference room while her business partner walked Barker home. He should have time to feed him before coming back for the meeting with DCI Hill.

Lynne had just cleared away the detritus of the day and laid out the special cups they kept for VIP clients when she was summoned by the somewhat haphazard buzzer that they shared with the other tenants of Minster Precincts.

"Sorry I'm so early. I had no idea how long to allow for rush-hour traffic, so I allowed twenty minutes more than the sat nav suggested," said Verena Hill, who was somewhat starkly but professionally turned out in a black two-piece with a white shirt, no visible jewellery.

Her breezy manner was somewhat atypical, thought Lynne, who, after a long career in the CID, would know about these things.

"That's absolutely fine," said Lynne, adding that John would be joining them soon.

"What about Barker? I'm dying to meet him."

Sally had insisted on including the border terrier in the 'people' section of the agency's newly created website, which had been set up to develop Lynne's expanding network of corporate clients who required her assistance with their executive recruitment programmes.

"I'm afraid that John has just walked him home for the evening, but if we do end up working together, I will make sure you meet him."

Lynne was about to offer refreshments when Tedesco's steady plod up the twisting staircase became gradually more audible.

Verena Hill rose to greet him, giving him what he would later describe as the firmest handshake he had ever received.

This was a good thing. His first impressions of Verena Hill were of a straight dealer, no messing, someone of quiet authority.

Lynne suddenly remembered the coffee, the offer of which was accepted by DCI Hill, who achieved another tick in Tedesco's box by taking it black.

Then the guest took charge of the meeting.

"So, cards on the table. We have your dead bishop, a plethora of crackpot theories ranging from divine retribution to a love triangle, all of which have been comprehensively discredited, and just some vague sightings of someone speeding away from the festival on a motorbike."

Lynne caught Verena's eye, then spoke up.

"The love triangle – were the other two sides of it the bishop's wife and the chief executive?"

"My, you guys are on top of things. Yes, it was Stephanie Walker and Keith Neighbour. But they both have alibis.

Neighbour was even spotted on film, writhing around with the other happy-clappers as if the second coming was minutes away. And Mrs Bishop was at home in the Cathedral Close, working on her lecture notes."

Tedesco smiled. He rather approved of DCI Hill.

Shame about the wedding ring though, he sadly noted to himself.

"Anyway. I didn't need Jimmy Bloomfield's glowing reference to know that the agency of Tedesco and Davey was responsible for solving the recent spate of murder mysteries down here – what is it about this place? It seems so calm and quaint on the surface – so I'm here to ask if you can help. Do you have any insight into who might have wanted to bump off a bishop of the established church?"

"Well, like any good detective, my first question is whether the deceased had any enemies," said Lynne.

"Bishop James has gone out of his way to alienate certain people," Tedesco added, "from LGBT+ Christian groups, to single mothers, through to many of our clergy and their congregations who have felt patronised and bullied by the new regime."

Verena Hill sipped her black coffee, then looked directly at Tedesco.

"None of what you say surprises me, John. But can you think of anyone – or a group of angry individuals – who might feel strongly enough to commit murder?"

Tedesco removed his glasses, polishing them vigorously before putting them back on again, which Lynne recognised as a classic sign that her colleague was having a deep think.

"Can I ask you something that's been bothering me, Verena? I don't think it's as simple as looking at someone who might want to silence the bishop. I gather that the way he was killed was very specific."

"We know about the carved letter on his back," Lynne continued.

"Okay, but what you might not know is that the letter wasn't carved. It looks like it might have been tattooed."

"How on earth would someone have the time to do that without being discovered?" asked Lynne.

DCI Hill took another sip. "The widow, Stephanie, is adamant that her husband didn't have a tattoo and we have drawn a blank with local parlours. The ink found on Bishop James was of a different type to the ones they normally use."

"Verena, do you have a picture of the letter 'A'?"

"Not that I can share with you, but it looks like something you might find on an old document, like an illuminated manuscript. What are you thinking?"

Lynne cut in. "I've just had an idea. John, doesn't the cathedral gift shop sell cardboard stencils that you can colour onto paper?"

"Brilliant! They do! I think they are based on the Rhyminster bible."

"So," said Verena Hill. "Who do I talk to?"

*

It was well into Autumn now, and dusk was falling as the three of them made their way to the cathedral.

Tedesco had remembered two things, firstly that there was going to be a preview for the cathedral's latest art exhibition that evening and secondly that the gift shop would be staying open late as a result.

There were already a few visitors to the preview wandering around the shop buying the brochure and other exhibition merchandise.

Lynne strode up to the till and asked the anxious-looking chap who was manning it if Andrea was in.

"Good, could you tell her that John Tedesco and Lynne Davey would like a minute of her time."

The flustered volunteer returned after a brief interval, accompanied by the petite figure of Andrea Hutchins, the manager, who Tedesco and Lynne had last seen after she had been winched down from the tower on the annual safety inspection.

"John, Lynne, the refectory is open late – shall we move through?" said Andrea, leading the way.

Approaching the entrance to the dining area they found that there were glasses of red and white wine laid out, together with the obligatory elderflower whatever for the abstemious and the motorists.

"The booze is for the VIPs, but I'm sure Tubbsy won't mind if we help ourselves," Andrea said, aiming her remark at Mark Tubbs, the refectory manager and a fellow survivor of the descent from the tower.

"Knock yourselves out," said Mark, adding that Jos Elsted had supplied the wine.

Lynne and Verena opted for elderflower: Lynne would be cycling, and Verena had a long drive home. Andrea said she would wait till the guests arrived.

Tedesco had no such excuse not to indulge, so eagerly scooped up a glass of red.

Having established from Mark Tubbs that the reception for the great and good would get underway in half an hour,

Tedesco introduced Verena Hill to Andrea, who looked understandably startled.

"It's okay, Andrea," Lynne reassured her, "you aren't being questioned or anything. We need your advice."

"Go on – you have got me intrigued now."

Tedesco spoke next. "I think I'm right in saying that the shop sells stencils of medieval writing and so on."

Andrea thought for a moment. "We used to, at least back in the day. There was a craze for brass rubbing a few years ago, heaven knows why, and these stencils seemed to be a spin-off from that. They also went down well with school trips.

"Look, let me see what I can find in the office, see who supplied them and if they are still available. Just one thing – why are you all so interested in colouring in? It seems more than a little bizarre."

Verena Hill stepped in. "Believe it or not, this could be important, so please keep it to yourself."

"I think I might join John in a glass of red after all…"

EIGHTEEN

The next morning, Tedesco's head was buzzing about Lynne's stencil theory and he was still worrying about Nicky and her divorce petition, so he headed out early for the service of morning prayer in search of some peaceful distraction.

"Good to see you, Mr Tedesco," said Colin the verger. "We are in St Nonna's chapel today. As the art exhibition is in the Lady Chapel, we can't use it this morning."

The lawyer turned detective didn't mind at all. The little side chapel was a special place to him, especially at this time of day.

As he waited for the service to begin he found himself drawn to the carvings of heads on the stone screen to his left.

One of the guides had told him that they were believed to have been carved by the masons who built the cathedral, possibly based on caricatures of each other, or maybe taken from faces of local people, or a combination of both.

He was particularly drawn to one of the faces.

It was of a man who appeared mellow – squiffy rather than drunk – as if he had just enjoyed a session of mead drinking with his mates. He rather liked this face. It reminded him of someone he'd seen, quite recently in fact. But who was it?

As the procession, consisting of Izzie the head verger and Canon Wilf Drake, entered the little chapel he focused his thoughts on the service and allowed himself the luxury of letting the beauty of the language flow over him.

Afterwards, he fell into step with Canon Wilf, who, to Tedesco's relieved surprise, didn't ask him about the murder of the 79th bishop.

"When are you going up to Yorkshire, John? It can't be long, can it?"

"Next week. It cannot come quickly enough as far as I am concerned."

"If you see them, give them my love, won't you?"

Tedesco and Barker had been invited by Bob and Hilary Dwyer, otherwise known as the 78th bishop of Rhyme and his wife, to stay at their cottage in Helmsley on the edge of the Nork Yorkshire Moors while Bob led a pilgrimage to Assisi.

The retired bishop had developed a useful side-line in lecturing on cruise ships and leading short pilgrimages, and Tedesco had indirectly benefitted by enjoying access to a regular holiday home.

Barker seemed to relish the break from his usual walks but found the North Sea a little chilly compared to the South Hams coast.

Exiting the cathedral via the old consistory court entrance, Tedesco bumped into Andrea Hutchins, who had just arrived at work.

"I like to get in a good hour before we open the shop – difficult to concentrate on stock levels and VAT returns once the punters arrive. I'm glad I caught you though. The suppliers I used for the stencils are still around. There isn't much of a demand from cathedrals these days, but they do still supply them to English Heritage."

Having thanked Andrea he carried on back to St Budeaux Place where he could enjoy a quick breakfast before walking Barker over to 4A Minster Precincts.

*

"Mr T!" trilled Sally. "Did you see it last night?"

"What did or didn't I observe, Sally? A meteor shower? The second coming? *The One Show*?"

"You are so funny sometimes! David Attenborough, of course! It got me thinking about what we can do. Did you look any further into solar energy?"

"It's on my to-do list. Listen, I do care about the planet, but right now I need to get some work done or else we won't have a roof to cover in hideous panels."

Lynne, arriving in her colleague's wake, caught the end of the exchange.

"I heard that, Sally. I'll have a quiet word with him, but we will have to cut him some slack. He's worried about Nicky, which always makes him grumpy, and he needs a holiday."

"Good job he's got one coming up then..."

NINETEEN

Tedesco liked an early start; his canine best mate liked them rather less.

The border terrier was somewhat staggered to find himself awoken from a pleasant dream involving chasing his favourite yellow tennis ball on the beach at Bigbury on Sea to be lifted into the back of the Lancia at insane o'clock.

It was 4.30am when they exited the liberty of the Close, Barker's human companion opting for Enya as his ethereal musical accompaniment.

After a couple of 'Penelopes', Tedesco felt that he had broken the back of the journey by the time they got into Derbyshire, so he decided that they had time for a decent lunch break.

He found a dog-friendly pub on the fringes of the Chatsworth estate, which boasted a large garden, and so they spent a pleasant hour before re-joining the M1, which proved to be less of an ordeal than on previous visits.

It was late afternoon when they reached Helmsley. Driving round its peerless market square, Tedesco felt that it was like being in an advert for Yorkshire Tea come to life.

Bob and Hilary's cottage was to be found just off the main road to Pickering, but within a ten-minute stroll to the square. It was a bit like St Budeaux Place, close to the action but just far enough away to be able to escape.

Hilary had left some home-made carrot cake, and some 'Dogdale' biscuits for Barker, so the two friends tucked in and then Tedesco unpacked.

Having successfully checked online to see if the little microbrewery would be open, he and an enthusiastic Barker headed out at the stroke of six.

The brewery had a few seats inside set aside for drinkers but the pair made for the spacious yard area and were soon joined by a mixed bag of thirsty walkers, as well as the locals.

Tedesco was halfway down his first pint of Yorkshire Legend when he saw one of the regulars approaching. Was this the face he had remembered when he saw the carving in the chapel last week?

"Aye up, Barker. How's life down south?"

The border terrier had fans wherever he went.

While Barker reacquainted himself with his friends in the north, Tedesco enjoyed a merry chat about the weather prospects for his stay.

The local consensus was that if he wanted to walk over the hills to Rievaulx then tomorrow was the best option, as rain was expected in the middle of the week.

After two pints Tedesco felt the chip shop calling and joined the queue at Deep Blue.

"I could grow to love this place, Barker," he said as they walked back to the cottage.

"Woof," said the terrier.

TWENTY

"High hills surround the valley encircling it like a crown. These are clothed by trees of various sorts and maintain in pleasant retreats the privacy of the vale, providing for the monks a kind of second paradise of wooded delight."

Walter Daniel, Infirmary Master at Rievaulx Abbey, 1167.

After the shock of the previous day's early start, and feeling tired from the journey, the two best buddies set off for their pilgrimage at nine, stopping only to pick up some rolls at the deli in the Square.

The walk, which Tedesco had undertaken with Bishop Bob on his first visit to Helmsley, was less than strenuous, the initial climbs being rewarded with stunning views back to Helmsley Castle.

This felt like it was going to be an epic. The sun was making a shy appearance from behind the clouds. As the path was walled in, Barker could be unleashed and Rhyminster, the agency and Nicky were soon safely out of reach and temporarily out of mind. But what was buzzing in his subconscious?

Van Morrison again: the spoken word 'Coney Island'.

As they descended into the valley he put Barker back on his lead, as they would be on the road for the last stretch. They were soon in sight of the River Rye, sparkling in the sunshine, and then the ruined Abbey came into view.

Tedesco, an inveterate list maker who made a chart or a league table out of everything, was trying to work out whether this was in his top ten all-time favourite views, deciding after careful consideration that it was a nailed-on top five.

He didn't need a guided tour as this was his third visit and, having secured some water for Barker from the nice lady in the gift shop, he remembered to call in on the way out in order to buy some postcards for the office.

He hated the settled trend for posting pictures on Facebook or whatever. If nothing else, you were advertising to the world that you were away. 'Hi, burglars, we're having a great time, help yourselves, go on, knock yourselves out.'

And he enjoyed writing cards, so the modern world should lay off and just let him be himself.

There were picnic tables laid out at convenient intervals, so he took off his rucksack and tucked into the filled rolls from the deli. One was pulled pork, the other tuna mayo. Not quite up to Jenks' standards, but not bad. He would suggest to Joan that they should do pulled pork. It might be a bit advanced though.

Barker was dozing off so he decided not to wake him for a few minutes, happy just to be in this tranquil place.

Bishop Bob had explained the significance of St Aelred, the best known figure to be associated with Rievaulx until former prime minister Harold Wilson took the name when he was elevated to the House of Lords.

Aelred, born in 1110, had trained as a diplomat, but having enjoyed contact with the Cistercians, and with the obvious attraction of Rievaulx, he decided to forsake court life for the austerity of the monastery, where he developed it as a spiritual centre.

Aelred was also a renowned writer, and one of his later works, *De Spirituali Amicitia* (On human friendship), has led, in our modern sexuality-fixated era, to various theories about him. Was he advocating close male friendship? Was he even endorsing homosexuality?

Scholarly scepticism about this notwithstanding, several gay-friendly Christian groups adopted Aelred as their patron saint.

The gift shop contained various items of merchandise celebrating 'our Aelred', so he had evidently become a local cult figure.

After waking Barker, and having enjoyed a wander around the ruins, Tedesco called in at the gift shop to choose his postcards.

As he queued to pay he suddenly remembered what Andrea had told him: the stencils were still being supplied to English Heritage. Rievaulx was an English Heritage site.

"I don't suppose you stock stencils, do you? You know, for colouring in?"

The volunteer assistant thought for a while, and then abandoned her post to take Tedesco to a display area that featured faux monks' habits, plastic swords, and all manner of medieval-themed tat – including stencils!

"Is this what you were looking for?" she said. "They are made specially for us, and they are ever so popular."

She handed Tedesco a medieval letter 'A', just like something from an illuminated manuscript.

"It's an A for Aelred, you see."

Tedesco bought two, just to be on the safe side. Then he texted Lynne and arranged to ring her at 5.30pm, before it was time to call in at the microbrewery again.

TWENTY-ONE

Lynne was still hard at work when her colleague rang. She had decided to stay behind and catch up with paperwork – as her yoga class at the deanery started at 6.30pm, there was little point in her going home first.

"You sound upbeat, Mr Tedesco?"

"Am I? It's probably the wonderful walk we did today. You must come up here, Lynne. Rievaulx is absolutely magical."

"Good to hear it – anyway, why did you feel the need to interrupt your holiday? Sally and I have got everything under control."

"I'm sure you have. Look, you remember our conversation with Andrea about the stencils?"

"Yes, but the shop doesn't stock them anymore."

"No, but some English Heritage sites do. And guess what I found in the gift shop at Rievaulx Abbey today?"

Lynne leaned back in her office chair and smiled to herself. *Let's wind him up.*

"I have no idea. I dunno, a flashing monk doll? A medieval recipe for Yorkshire pudding? Sean Bean buying some chutney?"

She could feel the irritation coming from down the line. "This isn't funny, you know."

She stifled a giggle. She knew he'd say that.

"Okay, so what exactly did you find?"

"The Abbey shop does stock stencils like Andrea's. They are made especially for Rievaulx."

"Don't tell me – they are in the form of a huge letter 'A'."

"They are, and the reason is the link to St Aelred."

"St Ale – something? What is he, the patron saint of beer guts?"

"Lynne. This is serious. I suggest that you do some research on Aelred. He was a fascinating person, with some ideas that were centuries ahead of his time. And he is seen in some LGBT+ circles as an inspiration for the acceptance of all forms of human sexuality."

Lynne paused. "Okay, I think I see where you are going. Bishop James was a strict traditionalist, who seriously upset liberal opinion. So are we looking for a group, or an individual, who used Aelred as a clue as to why they murdered him?"

"Maybe. I've bought a couple of stencils. I assume that the police and the medics can compare the template with the one on the body to see if they match. I assume we still have a body?"

"Yes, there's going to be an inquest. Look, I'm off to the deanery for Jo's yoga class. Should I try and have a quiet word with Dean Dan about your Aelred theory?"

Tedesco glanced at his watch. It would soon be opening time at the microbrewery.

"Hmm. On balance, why not? I'm no theologian. Just run the name past him and see how the conversation develops."

*

Lynne decided to go over to the deanery ten minutes early. The dean would be on his way back from the daily service of evensong and, if she timed it just right, she could snatch ten minutes with him.

She was in luck. "How was it, Dan?"

"We just about managed to pack them in – we were rammed to the gills. Must have been at least fifteen in the congregation."

"Any chance of a quick word before the yoga class?"

The dean quickly led her into his study.

"Okay," she started, "this may seem a bit left field, but John has been in touch from Yorkshire and he thinks that St Aelred may be a significant clue."

"It is somewhat out of the blue, as you say. St Aelred of Hexham, Cistercian abbot, and scholar, with some very modern ideas on the nature of true friendship. So, what has he got to do with Bishop James?"

Lynne did her best to explain Tedesco's theory, Dan's body language betraying first an instinctive scepticism and then a dawning realisation that he shouldn't simply dismiss the idea.

"Lynne, I'm hardly an expert on Aelred but I can think of someone who might be. Do you know Henry Easton?"

"Isn't he something to do with Lady Derrington?"

"In a sense, yes. He is the rector of Derrington and Hillbrook. And he runs the Street Pastors and has links to the annual Rhyme Pride festival. Could you be free later in the week if I arranged a little meeting?"

TWENTY-TWO

The Raven

Martin Clamp was on duty at the 8am service that fateful Sunday morning. The sidesmen were expected to turn up half an hour earlier and Clamp wisely decided to visit the loos, sited just off the cloisters, as he doubted if his bladder would hold up for the entire service, especially in the unseasonably cold weather.

After completing his ablutions, the sidesman turned in to the cloisters en route for the visitor entrance, when he became aware of a dazzling sensation, probably early morning sun.

A dark figure appeared from the light, a bit like a TV talent show contestant or a stand-up comic emerging from a fog of dry ice.

The figure approached slowly, before getting uncomfortably close. Clamp was too frightened to question this invasion of his personal space as he took in the stranger before him.

He was quite short but heavily built, dressed head to toe in black and he wore a prominent ring on his left index finger.

"Martin," the apparition said in a whisper. "You work for them. The dean and chapter."

"I'm a volunteer, so yes, in a way."

"I know everything about this place, Martin. You don't know who I am, do you?"

"Er, no…"

"I am the Raven."

Clamp was drawn to the man's ring, which was in the shape of a bird of prey.

Just as he wondered if this was a bad dream or how he could escape, he heard Canon Wilf.

"Good morning, Martin. Are you all right? You look as if you have seen a ghost."

TWENTY-THREE

The locals had been right about the weather. The next couple of days were almost complete washouts, so Tedesco made use of the excellent Helmsley community library in the Town Hall.

He left Barker to his own devices and splashed his way to the volunteer-run facility, where he was greeted with great warmth, the more so when he asked about the Abbot of Rievaulx.

"We've got a whole section on him and there's a lot you can find online, of course."

He settled down with a modern English version of the great man's spiritual writings, from which he picked out some key passages and quotes.

The abbot, he read in one of the commentaries, knew every one of the members of the community at Rievaulx by name, no mean feat as there were over five hundred of them, and Tedesco was particularly moved by one of Aelred's greetings: *'Here we are, you and I, and I hope that Christ makes a third with us.'*

He could just imagine his friend Canon Wilf coming out with that.

Reading more deeply into his subject he learned that whilst his ideas were influenced by his times – this was the age of the travelling troubadours and notions of courtly love – Aelred was just as influenced by his wide reading, particularly of Cicero.

Simply put, Aelred's ideal of friendship valued loyalty above all, which left the door open centuries later for the suggestion that he was relaxed about homosexual friendship – but Tedesco concluded from his research that the idea of spiritual friendship as described by the Abbot of Rievaulx was primarily firmly rooted in belief in a divine power.

'*Friendship will be full of riches for those who cherish it when it is completely centred on God*,' Aelred wrote.

How these gentle but powerful ideas could be twisted centuries later to justify murder was beyond belief – or was it? Buddhism had been used as a justification for ethnic violence in Myanmar, and history is littered with examples of the words of peacemakers being mangled in order to sanctify conflict.

All this deep thinking was making him hungry, so he decided to take Barker for a rainy walk followed by a pub lunch.

*

The dean didn't hang around, finding space in his busy diary by swapping an evensong duty with the precentor and persuading Henry Lawson that he could miss an ecumenical Churches Together gathering, just this once.

Lynne cycled along the busy Plymouth Road where she found the two clerics lying in wait in the garden of the River Hotel, a newly renovated place with gardens leading down to the River Rhyme.

The venue had the twin advantage of being just outside what passed for Rhyminster city limits and being sufficiently fresh-paint new not to have yet developed into a regular meeting place for cathedral types.

Lynne was greeted, somewhat conspiratorially, in the foyer, where Dean Dan whispered that he had secured a table in a little summer house facing the river.

"We will be safely out of earshot."

As the two clergy representatives were both driving and Lynne had the bike they all decided on soft drinks – although Henry was persuaded by the mocktail menu, opting for a flamboyant-sounding 'Ballsy Boatman'.

The dean started by explaining to the rector of Derrington and Hillbrook that John Tedesco had unearthed a potential link between the modern cult of Aelred and the death of Bishop James.

Henry took a sip of his suspiciously pink coloured mocktail.

"I think I get it now. I'm here as the Aelred expert.

"Lynne, Dan knows that I do have a devotion to Aelred and his concept of spiritual friendship. This came about through my work with the Christian Pride movement. Aelred has been taken up somewhat by such groupings and while on the one hand I think that trying to apply the writings of a medieval monk to the sexual politics of the present may be seen as naïve at best, then doesn't the same argument apply to seeking to relate the teachings of Christ to the 21st-century?"

Correctly sensing that Lynne wasn't quite ready for an evening seminar on theology, Dan brought the conversation back to the issue at hand.

"Henry, John has been staying at Bishop Bob's place up in Yorkshire and he and Barker walked over to Rievaulx Abbey."

The rector's eyes lit up. "Blessed Rievaulx – the lucky chap. I still haven't been there."

"Anyway, as I think you may have heard on the diocesan grapevine, poor Bishop James was found with medieval lettering engraved on his back…"

Lynne cut across the dean. "Except it wasn't engraved, of course. It was coloured in some way, probably spray-painted, using a cardboard template."

"Didn't they used to sell them in the cathedral?" said Henry.

"They did," Lynne replied, before going on to explain how Tedesco had unearthed an Aelred stencil with the invaluable assistance of Andrea at the cathedral gift shop.

"John is bringing the template back with him next week and then the police will ask the medics to compare it with the image on the bishop's back."

Dean Dan checked his watch, more out of habit than necessity. Having swerved evensong and with no meetings in the diary, he was enjoying a rare evening of freedom.

"What we want from you, Henry, is any insight you can offer us in the light of this development. We don't want to put you on the spot, but the kind of thing you might be able to help with is whether any of the Aelred-inspired groups have veered to the extreme in any way."

Henry Easton sighed before answering. "I will have a think and speak to people in those circles, but my gut feeling is to reject the idea of extremism. Aelred was advocating a peaceful, almost pacifist life."

He took another careful sip of his 'Ballsy Boatman' before continuing.

"Wait a minute. Lynne, you were at the vigil outside the North Canonry weren't you? And did I see you there as well, Dan?"

Lynne and Dan both nodded by way of confirmation. They had both been more than disappointed by the newly appointed bishop's express disdain for alternative lifestyles, as exemplified by his refusal to engage with Rhyme Pride, and had joined the silent protest outside the bishop's palace. Lynne happily recalled it as a dignified occasion, one that somehow managed to unite all aspects of Rhyme society from Lady Fiona downwards.

"Although it was a silent protest, there were quite a few banners – do you remember?"

Henry Easton was visibly racking his brain. "That's it! I remember now. One of the protesters was waving a flag which said something like 'Listen to Aelred'!"

Lynne gulped down some more overpriced San Pellegrino.

"I knew I'd seen that medieval lettering before. It was on that banner. The letter 'A.'"

The dean made as if he was about to ask them to join him in a prayer, Lynne looking mightily relieved when he didn't.

"I knew that you two would find a way through this. So, what we need to establish is the identity of the person with the banner."

Henry looked sheepish. "I know who it was. I can picture him now. It was Silas."

Before the rector could elucidate Lynne announced that she needed to go, as she would have an early start the next morning: she had pressing business in Bristol.

TWENTY-FOUR

She was so proud of him. For his part, Duncan Chivers knew that he wouldn't have had the confidence to apply for, let alone land, the vacant anchor role at Points West, the Bristol-based local BBC station, if Lynne hadn't entered his life at the precise moment she did.

Paul Simon: 'Born at the Right Time'. He'd even started to develop a Tedesco-style internal soundtrack to his life.

The cheerful reporter had been happily becalmed at *Searchlight* for years, succumbing as many before him to the seductive charms of the deep south-west at the risk of becoming nativist – not seeing the point of London, or foreign travel, as 'we've got it all down here'.

Then this amazing, funny, energetic whirlwind of a woman came out of nowhere and swept him off course.

They ordered their lunch starters, and then clicked glasses. Feeling a little giddy, they had opted for two glasses of house champagne to celebrate.

Looking out over the peaceful waters, Lynne felt that life couldn't get better, but she was painfully aware that some difficult conversations awaited them both.

Her sister lived here, so she had an approximate idea of the city, although she hadn't been to the Harbour House before. Bristol was becoming achingly cool, but she liked this place. The conversational hum was contented rather than smug.

Duncan gave her a playful nudge. "Away with the fairies?"

She smiled. "No, just happy and proud. But when are we going to tell the Tedescos?"

"Why don't we invite them out to supper and tell them both at the same time? It won't be easy, but at least we can do it together."

A familiar couple barged their way through the restaurant to a reserved table, which seemed to afford the best view of the painted houses.

The man was large, well-built wouldn't quite do him justice, with bushy eyebrows. The woman was, by contrast, thin but wiry, Lynne instantly clocking a fellow gym bunny.

Once they were seated at their table they looked up from their menus, and Lynne recognised them. It was Keith Neighbour and the bishop's less than grieving widow, Stephanie Walker.

*

Duncan and Lynne took a cab to Bristol Temple Meads in good time for the Plymouth Express. Lynne would be getting off at Rhyminster, while her partner would stay on for the next and final stop.

"I thought I recognised them," said Duncan as the train seemed to be in two minds before slipping into Taunton station.

"She works at the university, but not sure what the Neighbour from Hell was doing so far away from the diocese."

"They looked pretty 'neighbourly' together, don't you think?"

Lynne groaned, then added that her research into the late bishop had revealed that Keith Neighbour had been a protégé of Stephanie's old man.

"Ocker Walker? Do you think he was behind the takeover by the fundamentalists or whatever you call them?"

"Far-right Christian evangelicals. It is a theory. But right now, I wonder what is really going on between those two – and whether it was going on when Bishop James was alive."

*

Up in Yorkshire, Tedesco didn't let the weather get him down too much. He took Barker for a drive over to Whitby, which was more crowded than he might have imagined, and enjoyed some lung-busting hikes on the moors when the rain finally relented. On one of the walks, they crossed paths with a man with a familiar face. Could this have been the face he had seen on the carving in the cathedral? This was starting to really bug him.

He tried not to worry about Nicky – he was pleased that she had finally taken the plunge and petitioned Chag, presumably on the basis of his adultery with Rochelle, but he knew that the battle royale would be over the matrimonial home, Crane House.

And having finally accepted that Lynne and Duncan were in it for the long haul, he still fretted about what this meant for the agency, and Barker wasn't getting any younger…

It was time to get back to work. The few days away had done him good, he'd made a possible breakthrough by the happenstance of visiting Rievaulx, and he would soon be back up here. Helmsley was, he now realised, his unofficial second home.

"Come on, Barker, let's go down to the brewery for a final pint before we hit the road tomorrow."

TWENTY-FIVE

All were safely gathered in. Tedesco and Barker had returned from Helmsley, Lynne from Bristol, and Sally from her long-anticipated weekend at an Extinction Rebellion folk festival in Dorset.

Tedesco suggested a meeting at 10.30am, which should allow him time to catch up with his post and email – he certainly wasn't the type to log on when he was on holiday, that was one of the bugbears of his old career – and so Lynne told Sally to hold all calls.

After some routine pleasantries about his trip, Tedesco produced the stencil from his battered old briefcase.

"I've already booked a courier to pick it up and take it to the police, so Verena Hill will be on to it as soon as it arrives," said Lynne, before giving a summary of her meeting with the dean and Henry Easton.

Her colleague suddenly got up and walked around the room, a sure sign that some serious mulling was going on.

"Silas – now why does that name ring a bell? Silas Marner, of course… Wait a minute, I've got it! Bishop Bob had a gardener called Silas – do you remember?"

"I do – Hilary asked me to talk to him at one of the fetes held on the bishop's lawn – he was on his own, looking like a real Billy No-Mates.

I heard that he lived in a hedge until Bob and Hilary took him in"

"He was homeless, Lynne. Working for the bishop turned his life around. Bob told me that Silas had been in care and had spent years running away from authority and from a world that had turned on him both for his chaotic life and his sexuality. Bob found him a place on a gardening course at Rhyme College, and he never looked back – until Bishop James arrived."

"I assume that he was another casualty of the Neighbour from Hell?"

"I'm not sure where the lovely Keith would have put Silas on his spreadsheet, but it was Stephanie who really took against him, so I heard."

Lynne almost mentioned her surprise sighting of the late bishop's widow, realising just in time that this would prompt questions about what she was doing in Bristol. This would have to wait until she and Duncan had shared their news, a prospect she was dreading.

So, she switched tack. "Where is Silas now? Not living rough again, I hope?"

Tedesco stretched back in his chair. "No, the story ends well. Silas has been given a job at Derrington Hall, Lady Fiona is gushing with praise about the transformation he has overseen, and he's living happily in a tied cottage on the estate."

"Okay John, but do we really need to mention him to Verena? He clearly knows about Aelred and was waving a banner with the letter 'A' on it, for heaven's sake."

"Why don't you ask the good rector about him first? You said that Henry looked pretty sheepish when he mentioned his name."

"Good call. In the meantime, how would you like to come out for supper with me and Duncan?"

*

The courier duly picked up the package containing the Aelred stencil and successfully delivered it to the Bridewell, the main police station in Bristol.

The coming days would confirm that the template was an exact match for the one put to such gruesome use at the Soaked by the Spirit festival.

In the meantime, Nicola Tedesco was slightly taken aback to receive a call at work from her brother's business partner.

"Lynne! This is a pleasant surprise!"

"I hope this is a good time."

"Sure is. It's my turn to go through the daily weather photo submissions. You know the kind of thing – 'Dave from Saltash took this lovely but totally unoriginal view of the Tamar Bridge earlier today.'"

Lynne chuckled. The Tedesco siblings were very different, but they shared the same dry sense of humour.

"I was just wondering if you would like to come to supper with me and Duncan. John will be there too."

"Sounds good – why don't you text me some dates? I'm doing three evenings a week as the studio anchor, so I can normally make a Thursday or Friday. Good news about Duncan, isn't it? We will really miss him, as will our lovely viewers once we announce it. And what will you do? Are you going to move with him?"

Lynne ended the call, beating herself up for not thinking soon enough that Nicky would, obviously, know about Duncan's promotion. But had she confided in her brother?

TWENTY-SIX

The rectory at Derrington had somehow managed to survive the mass sell-off of Georgian vicarages that had taken place in the 1980s and beyond, thanks in no small measure to the fact that the parish church, and the neighbouring one in Hillbrook, constituted a benefice that remained under the patronage of the Derrington family.

Lady Fiona would never agree to 'her' rector living in a soulless box miles from the parish church.

"It is quite magnificent," Tedesco told Lynne as she was about to cycle off for her meeting with Henry Easton.

"It's like I imagine Ullathorne would be. I can just picture Septimus Harding calling in to visit the Thornes."

Lynne's expression told its own story: Tedesco really was losing it.

"You know – Trollope! *Barchester Towers*! Lynne, I can just about forgive your shocking ignorance of the songs of Nick Drake and Clifford T Ward, but you live in a cathedral city. Trollope is everywhere you look!"

"Oh yeah, I spotted him at Parkrun the other week with his gym buddy Charles Dickens. Must dash, don't want to keep the rector waiting."

*

The parish church of St Cyriac and the adjoining rectory sat proud of the modern village of Derrington, but within easy reach of Derrington Hall.

Lynne was greeted with great warmth by both Henry Easton and his equable border collie, who was introduced to her as Islay, named after the rector's favourite distillery.

"I inhabit two rooms downstairs, the kitchen and the study, and I make full use of the wine cellar. There are eight bedrooms, so I use most of them for waifs and strays."

"Was one of the strays called Silas by any chance?"

"I thought you would ask me that. Yes, Silas called one December evening in search of a bed for the night. He was in a terrible state, hungry, filthy, he'd been living rough for a long while. He'd learnt that the clergy were a soft touch, so he tried his luck with me."

"How long did you host him for?"

"Till after Christmas. I fed him up and he slept like a log while I was busy. Once he'd got used to me – Islay had worn him down much more quickly – he opened up about his life and said that he wanted to work in the outdoors. I knew that Bob needed help in the garden and now Silas is back here in the village working for Fiona and Edward."

"So I gather. Anyway…"

"You want to hear about Silas and his embrace of St Aelred. As you know, I run the Street Pastors in Rhyme – a refreshing, if challenging contrast to this parish. Silas trailed along with me once he was back on his feet, as much out of boredom as anything. He was really good with the kids we deal with, had real empathy."

"Am I detecting a 'but', Rector?"

Henry Easton smiled. "John told me that you would see through any attempt at obfuscation. Silas worked closely with a number of our volunteers but became particularly friendly with Jayne and Sean, who are both gay Christians, heavily involved in Rhyme Pride.

"One morning, Silas suddenly announced to me that he had become a Christian and that he had encountered Christ through meeting his new friends.

"Now he really believes that he was sent to Derrington in order to set off the chain of events that resulted in his being born again but, as you may have gathered from John, this brand of Christianity isn't one that I feel comfortable with."

"Not really my area, but surely someone like Silas would have been influenced by the kindness he received from different people – you, Bishop Bob and Hilary, Lady Fiona – who all happened to be Christians, rather than some sort of miracle or blinding light. That would be the logical view."

"You may have a point, Lynne. Anyway, Silas started to spend time with the gay Christian community and learned about Aelred, whom he started to venerate, hence the banner at the vigil."

"Could you imagine Silas feeling strongly enough to want to kill Bishop James?"

"No, he is a gentle soul really, if impressionable. But he was very angry indeed when Bishop Jim came out so strongly against the LGBT+ community. Silas had assumed that all Christians were as kind and open-minded as the ones he had met and so this was a real shock, almost a personal affront. It didn't help when Sean accused the bishop of effectively issuing a fatwa against minorities in Rhyme."

"Silly Sean, to put it mildly. But one thing bothers me, Henry. Could Silas, or maybe one of his new friends, have got hold of the stencil? I assume that whoever made that banner would have spray-painted the image on to it?"

"I will have a quiet word with Jayne next time I see her. She should know what happened to the banner. And unlike with Sean, I do trust her."

TWENTY-SEVEN

Diaries having been consulted, a mutually free Friday had become available and so John and Nicky Tedesco together with Duncan Chivers and Lynne Davey found themselves sharing a table at The Wild Bunch, Rhyme's newest independent eatery.

The owners were probably too young to remember the Sam Peckinpah film of the same name, but Tedesco was still disappointed by the distinct lack of Ernest Borgnine lookalikes present among the diners.

The closest match to a grizzled gunslinger he could spot was his old friend and colleague Neil Sparkes sharing a romantic dinner with his lovely wife Mary.

Tedesco waved over to them, and they merrily returned the gesture.

He was also aware of various grey-haired couples, all presumably loyal *Searchlight* viewers, nudging each other and whispering, "Is it them? You know – Nicola Tedesco and Duncan Chivers?"

A waiter emerged to explain the philosophy of the place: it celebrated the wild heritage of the area. The restaurant employed a forager to seek out natural ingredients from the plentiful array on offer and all their organic food was sourced from within a ten-mile radius.

All very right-on, but does it taste any good? thought Tedesco, wisely opting for silence.

He did, however, visibly roll his eyes at the vegan wine list, his sister throwing him one of her 'I know exactly what you are thinking, you miserable old git' looks.

"Well, this is all very nice," he said. "Nicky told me that we are celebrating something?"

Nicky and Lynne both looked as if they were about to choke on their samphire foam with foraged mushroom starters, but Duncan, in his usual reliable way, stepped up to the mark.

"We are, indeed, Mr Registrar," said the local-TV reporter, who was one of those who still addressed Tedesco by his former title.

He continued in a whisper, not wanting to be overheard by the *Searchlight* groupies.

"I'm moving up a notch. It's a bit like being promoted to the Championship."

Tedesco looked uncharacteristically foxed.

Lynne giggled. "Duncan is joining BBC West in Bristol – as the main presenter!"

The former diocesan registrar made a reasonably good fist of not looking upset.

"Not before time! I hope *Searchlight* got a transfer fee!"

Chivers, warming to the introduction of some football-related banter, responded that he'd been at his only club for so long that he had been granted a free transfer.

"Does this mean that I am losing you, Lynne?"

"Talk about taking down the vibe, bro," said Nicky.

Lynne, close to tears, stroked Tedesco's hand. "I will be moving to Bristol, yes. You know that I love the place, and it will be good to be near family."

Her colleague cut in. "But what will you do up there?"

"This is a celebration, John, so let's discuss this later. However, even you might have noticed that one can work from anywhere these days, so I'm sure we can sort something out."

The evening went a little downhill after that. Tedesco and Chivers bonded over Plymouth Argyle days of old, and long-forgotten names like Johnny Hore, Mike Bickle and Fred Binney started to ping around the table.

Meanwhile, Nicky opened up about her legal wrangles with Chag and how she had become a stronger woman now, wishing that she had left him earlier.

Lynne empathised, and then shared her guilt and anxiety over upsetting John.

"Your brother rescued me, Nicky. And now he feels abandoned. Look at him, it's like when Barker wears his sad face."

"John has always rescued me too, Lynne. It's what he does – but he was never going to commit, even to you. He will get over it. And he and Duncan seem to be having their own bromance."

Looking across the table, the two women witnessed a passionate debate taking place over who was the worst-ever Argyle striker, Tedesco being certain that it was someone called Jimmy Hinch, who Chivers claimed was well before his time.

"Time to go, I think," said Lynne, who had already prearranged for Mickey Hunn of Tower Cabs to pick them up. He would drop off Tedesco and Nicky, who was staying with her brother at St Budeaux Place for the night, before going on to Water Lane.

"What's this new place like, then?" said the ever-cheerful Mickey.

"I'd heard it was all weird stuff, no steaks or nothing."

*

Barker was asleep and Nicky wanted to go straight to bed, so Tedesco poured himself a glass of claret, as much to wash away the taste of the vegan Viognier as for the need of another drink and then he slunk down into his den.

After his usual rootle through his vinyl and CD library he found exactly what he was looking for, a very early Neil Sedaka/Howard Greenfield doo-wop collaboration: 'I Waited Too Long'.

"What am I going to do without her?" he said to himself, before checking on Barker and then tiptoeing quietly up the stairs.

TWENTY-EIGHT

At seven the next morning a groggy Lynne waved goodbye to Duncan, who was on sports desk duty at the Cornish Pirates, and then readied herself for Parkrun.

The minute she got out of the shower her mobile rang.

"Okay, okay, why can't you text like any normal human being!"

She picked up. "Oh, hello, Henry. I really hope that this is important."

The rector of Derrington and Hillbrook, slightly taken aback by the direct approach, hesitatingly apologised for calling at such an early hour, adding that he had some news for Lynne that couldn't wait.

"I was out with the Street Pastors last night and bumped into Jayne – you remember—"

Lynne cut in sharply. "Yeah, the girl who knows about the banner."

"Er, yes. Anyway, I asked her if she knew who made it and where it was kept now—"

Lynne, becoming even more impatient, asked him to get to the point.

"Well, here it is, you see. She told me that Sean and Silas had both worked on the banner and there had been some argument between them after the vigil as to who should keep it."

"Go on."

"Silas had been very insistent that he should have custody of the item, as he had somewhere safe to hide it."

The rector hesitated, so Lynne butted in again.

"Come on, Henry, if you know something."

"Silas told Jayne that he could hide it at Derrington Hall, which rather begs the question—"

"Why would he want to conceal it there unless he had something else to hide?"

Lynne then made a graceful apology for her rudeness, saying that she was not a morning person – a blatant lie if ever there was one – and thanked him profusely for the information.

She glanced at the clock on her phone. She had plenty of time to make the start of Parkrun, so she would make an early morning call on Tedesco and Nicky.

*

Nicky greeted her in her dressing gown at the door to Tedesco's cottage.

"If it's old grumpy chops you want to see, he's gone off to the paper shop with Barker, but I've got some coffee on the go if you've got time? I assume you are en route to Parkrun?"

After apologising for her brother's somewhat eclectic choice of mugs, Nicky poured out the coffee and then they sat together at the kitchen table.

"How is he today?" Lynne asked.

"He's got his sad little face on, and I heard him listening to some dreary old number about waiting too long just before I began to nod off."

Lynne quickly changed gear. "He will just have to get used to it. Bristol is on the train line and even John can cope with Zoom these days."

Nicky raised a quizzical eyebrow at this, but before Lynne could carry on, Tedesco came back from the paper shop with an excited Barker.

The border terrier liked Lynne, and he would miss her. It was a good job that dogs live in the moment or else he would have been as downcast as his master.

"John, as I was about to tell Nicky, I just wanted to see you before Parkrun."

Tedesco felt his heart jump – was she going to tell him that she'd changed her mind about Bristol?

"It's about the investigation."

"Oh, I see," Tedesco said, somewhat dolefully. "In that case…"

Nicky took the cue. "I need to jump in the shower and then I must get back to Woolford. Good to see you, Lynne."

Tedesco poured himself a black coffee and the two colleagues moved into the den.

Lynne gave a good precis of her conversation with Henry Easton, concluding with the revelation about the banner.

Her partner stretched, then spoke. "Is Henry going to approach Silas about this?"

"He thought that Lady Fiona might be the right person to ask – she is his employer, after all, and I think that she might handle matters with a bit more discretion, don't you?"

TWENTY-NINE

Lynne was in an uncharacteristically melancholy mood as she approached King George Field, the scenic starting point for the weekly work out.

How many more times would she enjoy this moment? *There will be Parkrun in Bristol, there are probably several, but it will be hard to replicate this.*

Sally, the agency's PA, was on the registration desk and Lynne greeted her warmly, a favour she hadn't always bestowed on the exhaustingly well-intentioned volunteer.

Her pal Jo, the dean's wife, was there, as, to her surprise, was the newish MP for Rhyminster, Raj Purbani, sporting some very expensive-looking and suspiciously clean running kit.

Fair play to him – at least he's getting involved locally, she thought, her reverie interrupted by the starting gun.

*

Meanwhile, over at Derrington Hall, Silas the gardener was surprised to be called upon by Lady Fiona in her weekend uniform of ancient Barbour, tweed skirt and sensible shoes.

"Ah, Silas, this won't take long," Her Ladyship said, letting herself over the threshold.

"I'm sorry at the state of the place – I was going to clear up later."

"Don't worry, I've seen far worse. It was about the vigil at the North Canonry. I had a question about that banner. We are holding a medieval-themed evening up at the Hall later in the year in aid of the diocese and their missionary link in Africa…"

Silas was like putty in Lady Fiona's elegant hands and he was only too happy to get the banner down from the barn in which it had been stored and to lend it to her so she could see if it sparked off some ideas.

"How did you manage to draw that marvellous letter? It looks like an illuminated manuscript?"

"It was easy really. I didn't draw it. I used a stencil, you see."

"How frightfully clever of you. And where did you find the stencil? I didn't know such things existed."

Silas looked down at the floor, clearly anxious at the turn of the conversation.

"I was only asking because it would be super if we could use something like that for our decorations for the medieval fair at the Hall."

Silas, discomfort personified, told Her Ladyship that he had worked on the banner with his friend Sean, and he would have to ask him about the stencil.

"Thank you so much, Silas. If your friend could point you in the right direction, I would be most grateful."

As soon as she made it back to Derrington Hall, Lady Fiona was reporting back to Henry Easton.

"I know Sean," said the rector. "He is an impressive young man in many ways, but a bit of an extremist. Fiona, you may have led us closer to the truth than you probably realise."

*

Martin Clamp looked out of his front window. His apartment was within what used to be the old Theological College in the Close and, although he didn't enjoy a view of the tower, he enjoyed more than a glimpse of the River Rhyme.

Early retirement from a career in senior retail management had led him back to the city of his birth, where he had made his bachelor existence tolerable by organising his life around North Rhyminster Golf Club and the cathedral.

He hadn't slept well since his encounter in the cloisters and the intervening days had given him cause for anxious reflection.

What had 'The Raven' meant by his sinister comments? Had Clamp just imagined it all? He didn't think so, but why did the man suddenly vanish when the precentor appeared?

Perhaps he needed to talk to Canon Wilfred about it? But would the precentor think him insane?

THIRTY

If it was to have been Lynne's final Rhyme Parkrun, then she had finished on a high, a personal best.

She felt her mobile vibrating, so wandered outside – it was too noisy in Starbucks, where the post-run chatter was in full swing.

It was Henry Easton.

"Henry! Two calls in one day!"

"Indeed. Look, I know you are busy, but Fiona has reported back. She called on Silas and he showed her the banner."

"Did she say if he was reluctant to let her see it?"

"No, he was a bit surprised to be asked but then he took her to the barn and displayed it to her."

"But that girl – Jayne? Hadn't she said that Silas was a bit off with her? And with Sean."

"In a manner of speaking. She was clearly a bit taken aback by how determined Silas was to gain custody of the banner. I was rather expecting Fiona to meet with more resistance."

"So, we have drawn a blank," said Lynne, clearly disappointed.

"Not entirely. Silas denied any knowledge of the source of the stencil and suggested that Sean would know as he had worked on the banner with him."

As she went back inside, Lynne wondered about whether Jos Elsted might be a good person to talk to – he was another street pastor and he'd have come across Sean.

Meanwhile, there had been a surprise development from the organisers of the Soaked by the Spirit festival.

The Avon and Somerset police had, to date, obtained no useful leads concerning the motorbike that had been seen speeding away from the showground while the worship band had been playing.

Then, out of the blue, in the light of the evening, a young man called Tim Goodacre strolled into his local police station.

Tim looked as if he was born to wear a festival lanyard, his rather too direct stare exhibiting the zeal of the convert.

He had something important to show the police, and it related to the murder of the Bishop of Rhyminster. The desk sergeant, correctly assessing that the earnest young man before him was no time-waster, made a call to the Bridewell HQ.

Eventually, after a long wait, Tim was told that DCI Verena Hill was ready to speak to him.

The fresh-faced young Christian was led into the staff room, which had been tidied in honour of the senior officer.

Verena, wearing a tracksuit and expensive trainers, introduced herself, then apologised for keeping him waiting.

"It's a day off, but as this concerns the events at the festival I came in as soon as I could. I gather that you have something to show us?"

Tim produced an envelope. "This was brought in to the site office by a man on a motorbike, a courier."

"I see, and can you describe the man?"

"No, not really, he kept his helmet on. I do remember that he seemed quite slight, not a large person. He just left the envelope and said it was for the bishop. I clean forgot about it until I heard one of your appeals."

"How come you have it, Tim?"

"Oh, that's easy. I should have explained. I was in charge of the VIP area, looking after the acts and the guest speakers. I took delivery of the item, and would have handed it to the bishop, but..."

"He was killed. Okay, Tim, but what did you decide to do with the package?"

"Oh, well, I must have taken it home after the festival. I found it when I was rummaging for a clean pair of socks."

Verena allowed herself a smile. He was completely without guile and was telling the truth, surely.

"And what is in the envelope?"

"I don't know – I haven't opened it. It was private."

THIRTY-ONE

This was his chance. Martin Clamp was on the rota to steward the evensong service in the cathedral and the vestry had confirmed that Canon Wilf would be there.

As he wandered over to the cathedral, Martin told himself not to feel embarrassed. He knew what he had seen and the precentor wouldn't treat him like a fool.

Martin was in luck – Canon Wilf made a beeline for him as he stood at the entrance to the quire.

"Good evening, Martin? Are you feeling all right? You just look a bit anxious if you don't mind me saying. Look, do you need to dash off after the service?

"Why don't we have a chat in St Nonna?"

The sidesman was amazed at how Wilf could remember the name of every single volunteer, and even more taken aback by how the precentor seemed to have already known that he needed to consult him.

The service went to plan, the girls' choir was in superb form, and there was a respectable number in the congregation.

After clearing his area of stray prayer books and hymnals

once the service had ended, Martin wandered over to the tiny chapel where Canon Wilf was already waiting for him.

"Martin. Why don't you share whatever is on your mind?"

After a stumbling start, and with the precentor's kindly encouragement, Martin managed to relay the story of his encounter with the sinister 'Raven', ending with how he evaporated into thin air when Canon Wilf arrived.

"It took real courage for you to tell me about this, Martin. It may surprise you to learn that what you have just told me is by no means a unique tale. Buildings like ours attract strange characters, both physical and, I believe, in spirit form. From what you have recounted I think this person was real and highly skilled in the ancient art of putting the wind up folk."

"He certainly succeeded," said Martin.

"Leave it with me, and with God," Wilf said.

"I will ask around but, in the meantime, please don't worry any more. It's out of your hands now."

It was a Saturday night, so Wilf decided to start with the Street Pastors.

Just as that group of brave souls were gathered in prayer before venturing out to minister to the night-time economy, DCI Verena Hill had put gloves on before carefully opening the envelope intended for the late Bishop of Rhyminster.

It contained no note, card, or letter. The sole item within was a piece of cloth. Using tweezers to turn it over, she saw what it was. It was the same medieval letter 'A' that had been found on the bishop's corpse.

THIRTY-TWO

It was a dank early Saturday evening in the city centre, that no man's land between the end of the retail day and the start of the night-time economy.

The Rhyminster Street Pastors were gathered in the Baptist Church on Lower Jewry Street, gearing themselves up for the task ahead.

Unlike a sports team listening to an inspiring talk from the manager, this squad prayed together, seeking Christ's presence 'this night' in guiding them in their duty and asking him to look down favourably on the people they would encounter.

Before the brave volunteers ventured out onto the mean streets of Rhyme, Jos Elsted managed a quick word with Sean.

"Bit left field, I know, but did you and Jayne work on the banners we used at the Pride Vigil?"

The normally confident young man morphed into a slippery Dickensian mudlark.

"Who wants to know? Look, man, we need to get moving. The fleet will be here any minute."

'The fleet' was the pastors' shorthand for the convoy

of cars, motorbikes and taxis that descended on Rhyme every Saturday night, bringing in kids from the villages and a peppering of naval ratings from the onshore base at Stoneport, about fifteen miles away.

Jos stood his ground. "It is a long shot, but the diocese is having a medieval fundraiser to raise funds for medical support in Africa, and I thought of the gothic script that had been used on our banners. It might be appropriate to decorate the hall where the event is taking place."

"Look, Jos, we just used a crappy old stencil to spray paint the letter 'A' to make it look like ancient script. I've no idea where we got it from. Maybe Jayne can help you?"

"Okay – but you do agree that there was more than one banner?"

Sean's expression went beyond shifty. "Yeah. But so what?"

Jos wasn't the only amateur detective going undercover with the pastors that night.

While Lynne Davey had asked the kindly wine merchant to see what Sean knew about the banner, Canon Wilf, true to his word, had changed out of his clerical garb and cycled into town to lend his support to the pastors.

The weather had taken a nasty turn, which meant that there was a high demand at the soup tent.

The wintry blast, while keeping down the volume of clubbers, had had the opposite effect on the number of homeless people who were seeking warmth wherever they could find it.

"Ray, isn't it?"

Canon Wilf recognised one of his fellow ladle-wielding volunteers, a Falklands veteran who had fallen upon hard times, but who had gradually turned things round for himself, becoming a regular local character when he sold the *Big Issue* in Broad Street.

"Good to see you, vicar. You still working for the big boss?"

Having established that Ray was now happily settled with a widow in Castle Court, but that he still kept his ear close to the ground, Canon Wilf chanced his arm.

"Ray, bit of a strange one, but have you heard of someone calling himself 'The Raven'?"

The old sea dog looked as if he'd seen a ghost.

"Are you all right?" asked the canon precentor.

"Er, yeah. Just, like, I wasn't expecting that. I haven't heard that name for a fair few years."

Wilf kept silent, correctly assessing that Ray would want to unload.

"This Raven mush. Bloody terrifying, he is, appears out of nowhere, scares the hell out of you, pardon my French, then just as quickly he's gone into thin air."

"Do you know where I could find him?"

"I wouldn't advise it, but he tends to hang out with the crusties and the woo woo brigade over at Rhyminster Ring, seems to think he is the guardian of the place. He prowls around there with his dog, ugly thing, like the one Bill Sikes had in *Oliver!*, if you get my meaning."

Canon Wilf smiled reassuringly. "You've painted a vivid picture, Ray. You probably wonder why I've asked you about this man."

Ray nodded, somewhat nervously.

"Well, someone calling himself the Raven recently appeared in the cathedral cloisters and traumatised one of our volunteers."

"So, you thought you would try the Street Pastors? I'm glad I could help, but, vicar?"

"Ray?"

"Be careful. You don't know what you are getting into. That guy is seriously weird."

THIRTY-THREE

After relishing his routine walk to the paper shop with Barker, Tedesco decided that a visit to the cathedral for the service of Sunday Eucharist would be in order.

It was a bit long and busy for Barker, who seemed more than happy to have an easy Sunday morning. After all, he was a full-time pet and companion, 24/7 and 365 days a year, so he deserved a chance to chill out while his master went to church.

The detective was motivated less by devotion than curiosity. There were various threads emerging from the investigation, and, as well as the magnificent building being a good place to sit and think things through, there was a fair chance that he might pick up some insights from his fellow worshippers.

His instincts were spot on. Jos Elsted was on sidesman's duty outside the main visitor entrance.

Despite his walkout during the bishop's enthronement, Jos remained loyal to the dean, and, deciding that Dan needed all the support he could get, he continued as an active member of the Guild of Sidesmen.

"Jos! Have they put you on the naughty step this morning?"

"Not sure if this is the real naughty step – I think that might be the South Transept! Are you staying for coffee, John?"

Tedesco grimaced at the thought of the disgusting Fairtrade brew served after the service. He was all for supporting the third world, but did it have to be at the expense of decent coffee?

"You've got me intrigued – I'll see you after the match!"

"Ha ha. Only you could describe the act of worship as a match, Mr Registrar!"

Having resolved the quire/nave dilemma in favour of the nave today, Tedesco took his seat and read the printed notice sheet. It never ceased to amaze him how many good works sprang from this place. As well as the Food Bank and the Street Pastors, the notice sheet advertised various prayer groups, a campaign to raise awareness of prisoners of conscience and a peace vigil for Ukraine.

He enjoyed the service, and the dean gave a thought provoking sermon, but Tedesco still felt the familiar pang of unease as the moment came for the handshake of peace.

Whilst he had no time for the anti-handshake ultras, like Commander Foster, who saw the introduction of the 'sign of peace' as tantamount to heresy, or at least evidence of suspect underground beatnik tendencies, the detective had to admit that he had never felt quite comfortable about it.

It just didn't seem very British, really. We don't offer each other 'peace' when we meet, do we? We say 'good morning?', or 'how are you?', or 'all right, mate?'

And the random nature of the ritual was an issue. He genuinely wanted the best for most people in the congregation, but the last thing he wanted to wish someone like the Master of Musick was peace.

"Let us offer each other a sign of peace," intoned Canon Wilfred, who deliberately made a beeline for Tedesco, gleefully aware of how uncomfortable his friend would be as he shook his hand with exaggerated firmness.

Probably serves me right, Tedesco thought, then as he noticed that Lady Fiona was sitting behind him, he turned round and pointedly wished her a good morning. She smiled, clearly taking a similar line.

As the service ended with an organ voluntary, he and Her Ladyship strolled to the Chapter House, where coffee and biscuits were served.

"I had a word with Jos on the way in," said Lady Fiona, in her customary cut-glass tones. "You know that I visited Silas the other day."

"To ask him about the banner."

"That's right. Anyway, Jos met Sean last night at the Street Pastors, and managed to get him to admit that there was more than one banner. Jos tipped me off by text, so first thing this morning I went to the barn where Silas had shown me the one he'd been looking after, and guess what I found?"

"The other one, I assume."

"Of course – but the letter 'A' had been cut out, so this banner had a hole in it."

Jos joined them, fresh from his duties.

"I just caught the end of that. The obvious question is, why didn't Silas show you the other banner as well?"

"Perhaps he didn't see the point," Lady Fiona said. "After all, I had asked him about the script, suggesting that we could do something similar for the medieval evening at the Hall."

"Fair enough," said Tedesco, "but why do you think Silas kept the mutilated banner? You'd think he would just dispose of it, surely?"

THIRTY-FOUR

As he made his way back to St Budeaux Place, Tedesco stopped to check his phone.

Verena Hill had texted him during the service. He decided to call her back, and so he stopped at his special bench in the Close, donated in memory of Leslie Thomas, one of his favourite authors, who had lived in Rhyminster for a number of years. She picked up on the third ring.

"Mr Tedesco. Sorry to disturb you on a Sunday morning."

"Sorry I couldn't talk – I was in church."

"Oh, I see," said Verena Hill, sounding almost as surprised to hear that Tedesco had been taking place in an act of worship as if he had disclosed to her that he'd been enjoying a Sunday morning threesome.

"Anyway," she continued, "I had a meeting with a member of the public last night, a chap who was working at that Christian rave where the bishop was killed."

"And can you give me the gist of what he said?"

"What I think I can tell you, as you may be able to help us here, is that he produced an envelope containing a piece of cloth which displayed the same letter 'A' that was discovered on the bishop's back."

"And as I tracked down the source of the stencils, you thought I might have some amazing insight into this mystery piece of cloth?"

"Well, er…"

"Sorry, I'm being annoying, because the thing is, I have just found out that a banner has been discovered in a barn in Derrington from which the centre has been carefully cut out. And I am as sure as I can be that the symbol that was removed was the Aelred 'A.'"

*

At first light that morning, the two young, uniformed officers had found themselves climbing the gentle but lengthy incline leading from the village of Rhyme Margrave to the ancient site of Rhyminster Ring.

Jade Pollard and Tom Stocker had been briefed overnight, after Canon Wilf had been in touch with DCI Bloomfield about the Raven and Ray's insight as to his likely whereabouts.

As they circled the magnificent earthwork, Pollard became aware of a presence by her side.

"Jade. I know who has sent you."

Stocker was rooted to the spot, as if turned into a pillar of salt.

The apparition pointed to the distant tower of the cathedral.

Pollard, quite reasonably spooked, nervously addressed the black-clad stranger.

As she began to do so, a ferocious-looking bull terrier appeared at the man's side and then trotted towards PC Stocker, staring at him intently.

"What is your name, sir?" asked Jade.

"I know your name, Jade Pollard, so you tell me mine."

"Mr Raven, I believe."

"The Raven. And you want to ask me about down there," he said, indicating the cathedral.

"I would like you to come into the station and answer some questions about a complaint we have received."

"I'm sure you would. But, pretty little Jade, I do not recognise temporal authority."

The bull terrier snarled at PC Stocker, as he was calling for back-up.

"There's no need for back-up, Tom," said the Raven. "Grebo is harmless.

"You just ask me anything you want to and then go back down to the accursed city of the minster."

The Raven, still refusing to give any other name or a permanent address, remembered his meeting with Martin Clamp, stating that he was in the cloisters in his angelic capacity, protecting vulnerable souls like Martin from the evil spirits at large in the cathedral.

"But how did you know his name? Or mine? Or my colleague's?"

"Well, Tom. Bit of a secret. You see, the cathedral volunteers have these things called name badges. And you lot have your names on your coats, don't you? And I can hear you when you talk to each other."

PC Stocker, about to raise his voice, was shushed by Jade Pollard.

"All right, sir, you have had your bit of fun. But a word of warning. If we find out that you have been scaring volunteers again, then we will arrest you. Got it?"

"Oh aye, I got it all right. Anyway, Jade, here's something for you. A prophecy. A warning. A large beast from the ends of the earth is down there" – he pointed at the cathedral tower – "and it has already devoured its prey."

Once they were safely back in the patrol car, Stocker blew out his cheeks and then exhaled. "Christ almighty. What a terrifying bloke. And who the hell calls a pet dog 'Grebo'?"

"He seemed pretty tame to me – and the dog. But what did he mean about the large beast?"

THIRTY-FIVE

The next morning, DCI Hill sent two scene of crime officers to Derrington Hall, where they had prearranged to meet Lady Fiona.

They carefully compared the piece of cloth that had been couriered to the Soaked by the Spirit festival with the mutilated banner. Not only did the material match, but the symbol fitted perfectly in the hole that had been made in the banner.

Both pieces were taken to the lab for testing.

Later that day, a bewildered Silas agreed to go to Rhyme police station to assist the police with their enquiries, where he agreed to be fingerprinted on the grounds that he had nothing to hide. Sean and Jayne proved less cooperative.

Meanwhile, back at the medieval tower block that housed Tedesco and Davey's office, the retired lawyer updated his colleague on the weekend developments.

"You have been busy, Mr T. Let's look at this though. Why would someone send a courier with an envelope containing the same sinister one-letter message that was found on the poor old bishop?"

"I know, Lynne, it seems bizarre. Was it a warning? If so, it didn't work. Or was it some perverted game of double bluff? Anyway, we will see if the fingerprints provide any clue.

"In the meantime, Canon Wilf has summoned me to the refectory at half past ten."

"Don't be tempted by those Danish pastries."

"What, and spoil my appetite for some Jenks lardy cake later?"

An hour later, Tedesco headed down the death-trap staircase and then out into the Close. The boys from Bishop Lunt's school were on their break and so the tranquillity of the Close was spoiled for him somewhat by shouts of "Watkins, you spanner!" and "Give us back my homework, you total loser."

The refectory was somewhat steamy, full of tourists and tour guides sheltering from the blustery conditions.

Tedesco waved at Andrea Hutchins. She was sitting with one of the guides who was slightly desperately plugging his latest historical book about the cathedral, and then he spotted Canon Wilfred, who had commandeered a quiet booth near the loos.

"I've ordered some Minster Blend – I hope that's okay?"

"Minster Blend is always okay, Canon Precentor.

"So," Tedesco whispered, "is this about you know what?"

"Tangentially, yes. This business is getting so tangled up that I can't remember if I've discussed the Raven with you."

Tedesco made a 'search me, squire' gesture, and then Wilf summarised the version of events relayed to him by Martin Clamp, going on to explain that DCI Bloomfield had got back to him in the light of the informal interview on Rhyminster Ring.

The detective rolled his eyes, and then gave a world-weary sigh.

"How did the apostle put it – 'This may be a true saying worthy of all men to be received but in this case it's a load of old bollocks'?"

The precentor smiled indulgently. "I'm glad to see that you are at least half tuned in to the liturgy, and I understand your cynicism, but I have heard from two witnesses, Martin Clamp and Ray of *Big Issue* fame, and they were both taken in by this Raven character – and those young PCs were pretty shaken as well."

"Fair enough, but how does this weird black-clad Johnny Cash lookalike relate to the death of the bishop?"

"I'm not saying that he does, but just think for a second about his comment concerning a beast coming from the ends of the earth. Could he have been referring to Australia?"

"Come off it, Wilf, what do you mean, Men at Work: 'Down Under'?"

"Yes, in a way. Keith Neighbour is a large specimen – you might describe him as a beast – and he comes from Australia."

"Granted, but what about that bit about devouring his prey? I know he's effectively sacked a few priests and pushed Amanda out, but how would the Raven know about that?"

"You may laugh, think I'm off my rocker, but this area is ancient and full of strange figures with spiritual insights. All I am asking is that you keep an eye on the Neighbour from Hell. What do we really know about him?"

THIRTY-SIX

Silas was less than thrilled to be interrupted as he was cutting back the Japanese anemones, but he agreed to accompany the officers to the nearest station, Rhyminster, where he was cautioned and advised of his right to a solicitor, which he declined as he said that he had nothing to hide.

It was gently explained to him that his fingerprints had been found on the fragment of cloth taken from the second banner he was storing at Derrington Hall, and that the very same fragment had been couriered to the Soaked by the Spirit festival.

DCI Verena Hill, watching through the one-way glass, noted to herself that the suspect seemed genuinely flummoxed by the line of questioning.

When asked to account for his movements on the day of the killing, Silas was certain that he had been looking after Derrington Hall, as Lady Fiona was away in Somerset that evening, and he offered both Lady Fiona and Rev. Henry Easton as witnesses who could corroborate his alibi.

He had no knowledge of the whereabouts of the knife used by the murderer, but he was on more shaky ground when it came to the banner, at first denying any knowledge of the 'A' symbol having been carefully removed before changing his mind when the absurdity of his denial was pointed out to him.

He eventually revealed that the symbol had been removed by him at the express wish of Jayne and Sean, who had both been 'funny' about Silas storing the banners.

"You won't let them know that I dobbed them in, will you?"

He was released pending further enquiries, which would amount to a visit to Derrington to call upon Lady Fiona and her rector.

So, early the next morning, Her Ladyship was somewhat startled to be confronted by DCI Hill and a colleague as she was about to set off on her daily walk with the dogs.

Having checked her diary, she was able to confirm that she had been in Somerset on the day in question. As she was staying the night with friends she had asked Silas to look in at the Hall and check that all was well, draw the curtains and so on.

"You of all people will know about the increase in rural crime, officer," she added.

Lady Fiona wasn't quizzed about the purpose of her visit, which came as a relief to her as the last thing she needed was to try to explain about the meeting at Mells, not least the comments about the turbulent bishop.

Hill thanked her but wasn't prepared to write Silas off just yet. Her Ladyship hadn't really accounted for his movements, only confirmed the contents of her instructions to her gardener. She had no means of knowing if he had been at the Hall all day, assuming that the ancestral home lacked CCTV.

Having established that the rector would be found in church after morning prayer, Hill and her junior officer caught up with him.

Henry was a little more persuasive than his patron, making the point that Silas had no means of transport other than an ancient bike that he had discovered in one of the outbuildings, which meant that if he had been to the festival site he'd have needed a lift there and back again.

He also felt 'sure' that the gardener would have followed his employer's instructions to the letter.

As DCI Hill knew they would, Lady Fiona and Henry Easton were soon to be found comparing notes and the latest news would soon be winging its way over to Minster Precincts.

THIRTY-SEVEN

Tedesco spent a frustrating early evening carefully transcribing the latest revelations into his case book.

He couldn't visualise poor old Silas as being other than an innocent accomplice of Sean and possibly Jayne. He hadn't met either of them, but Henry Easton clearly regarded Sean as a hothead and an extremist. If he was, then things could get difficult for the gardener.

And try as he might, he couldn't forget what Wilf had told him about the Raven. From anyone else it would be preposterous, but he trusted his friend's instincts. And what *about* Keith Neighbour? Again, he had experienced next to no dealings with him, but the reports were consistent – the man was physically intimidating, ruthless and by all accounts charmless.

But he was Bishop James' right-hand man, so why would he wish his boss harm when their futures were inextricably linked, at least in the medium term?

And what did Keith know about Aelred, assuming that the medieval monk was central to the investigation, as he must be, surely?

The 'A' on the bishop's back, the banner, the package delivered to the festival site. It must all mean something.

As he was getting nowhere, Tedesco fixed himself some pasta, uncorked a bottle of Jos Elsted's burgundy and settled in for a night with his vinyl collection.

After a while he realised that he was working his sad way through the alphabet of wallowing classics, from 'Alone Again (Naturally)' through Linda Ronstadt's killer version of 'Long, Long Time' to 'Solitaire'. This wasn't good.

"Come on, Barker, let's go for a night walk."

Meanwhile, at Crane House in Woolford, another Tedesco was drowning her sorrows.

Nicky had just heard from her solicitor that her husband's business was in trouble and that the bank was calling in his debts. And the major asset that secured the borrowings was the matrimonial home. The solicitor was seeking counsel's opinion on a possible case against the bank for failing to insist on Nicky receiving independent advice, but this would cost her more money and the bank would no doubt mount a robust defence. Chag was clearly in denial, carrying on as if nothing was wrong, planning a new life with his much younger partner.

How would she manage? She would keep working, but how could she support the kids? Where would they live? Jack was at university, but these days, unless they got a job with a hedge fund, adult children tended to boomerang back to the family home. She wondered whether John could take them in, although he would hate the loss of privacy. *Barker would be more understanding*, she thought with a smile.

And over at Water Lane, a sober Lynne suddenly remembered that there was something she hadn't mentioned to her colleague. She tried calling, wondered what he would be doing out on a school night, then settled in with some old episodes of *Friends*.

She needn't have worried about John. He and Barker enjoyed an invigorating walk around the floodlit close, Tedesco noting that there was a light on in the North Canonry – *probably for security*, he thought.

There was a message awaiting his return, but he ignored it. The new morning would arrive soon enough.

THIRTY-EIGHT

Checking his messages after breakfast, and seeing that the latest was from Lynne, he decided against calling back as he would soon be seeing her in person.

As if on cue, she was awaiting him in the little interview room when he and Barker arrived at the office.

"Did you get my message? And where were you, dirty stop-out!"

"I took Barker for a late stroll around the Close. Nothing more than that."

"Bit touchy today, aren't we? Look, I suddenly remembered that there was something I didn't tell you which might have a bearing on the Jim Il Sung case."

"Withholding evidence from your partner, Mrs Davey?"

Lynne silently screamed. What was wrong with the man?

"If you let me explain. It was before you found out about my move to Bristol with Duncan, and if I had told you about what I saw then you would have asked what we were both doing up there during the week."

"Hmm. So, you deliberately kept me in the dark. Okay, you'd better tell me."

"Duncan had just been told that he'd got the Points West job and so we went to celebrate at a really nice bistro near the harbour. I think you would approve. Anyway, I saw a couple I recognised from Rhyminster."

"Go on, who was it? Charlie Tantum and one of the Ladies of the Close…"

"Not remotely funny. It was Keith Neighbour and the bishop's wife."

"What the hell were they doing in Bristol? It wasn't in the diocese of Rhyminster last time I checked!"

"Well, Stephanie Walker teaches at the university, so she had a reason for being there, but heaven knows what the Neighbour from Hell was doing away from Rhyme."

"Hang on, Lynne, didn't you unearth some photos of them both back in Oz when they were younger?"

"I did – and I remember you making some lame joke about how neighbourly they looked."

Tedesco pretended to look crestfallen.

"I think it was an example of my incisive wit, Lynne. But this could be important. Wilf told me that one of the volunteers had been spooked by a strange chap who hangs out at Rhyminster Ring, and this oddball had warned the police about a beast from the ends of the earth who was at large in the cathedral, or words to that effect."

Lynne stifled a giggle, then said, "So you think he might have been referring to Keith?"

"Well, after what you have just told me, perhaps we need a closer look at the man from down under."

*

As Verena Hill had correctly predicted, the Rhyme bush telegraph was soon humming.

After finishing with Tedesco, Lynne was told by an excited-looking Sally that Her Ladyship wanted a call back and that it was urgent.

Lynne, the Guardian-reading woke leftie, and Lady Derrington, the true blue Tory, had struck up a long-running friendship over the years, and so it was no great surprise to ex-DS Davey to hear that Lady Fiona had called.

"Fiona. I gather we need to speak."

"Lynne, thank you so much for taking time out of your busy day. I know, of course, that you and John are taking an interest in the recent appalling event for the dean."

"Fiona, I know all about the Escape Committee, so you can speak freely."

"I had rather assumed you would. Anyway, Silas, my gardener you know, was hauled in for questioning. The police found his fingerprints on the banner that was cut up."

"Yes, John told me that the letter 'A' had been carefully removed."

"Good, anyway, they have let Silas go for now but he told them that he had been told to remove the symbol by two of the street pastors."

"Sean and Jayne?"

"I think so."

"Poor Silas. Leave it with us, Fiona. I will see what I can find out about those two."

THIRTY-NINE

Lynne tracked down the two young street pastors through Henry Easton, promising him that she would just be carrying out some background checks. Their full names were Sean Treagust and Jayne Rice-Foxton.

Making use of her investigative skills and the background checking software she used for her executive recruitment work, she soon established that they had both been involved in peaceful protest, such as campaigning against the Afghan war, nuclear weapons, and road building, as well as some more serious incidents of statue toppling.

They were both seemingly motivated by faith, as expressed by their work in the community, and neither of them seemed to be in full-time employment.

However, a quick Google search revealed that the Rice-Foxton family were seriously wealthy from the sugar trade and so Jayne was, quite probably, a trust-fund babe.

Sean's background had been more challenging, including periods of his early life when he had been in and out of the care system.

The police would presumably come calling on them after

Silas had 'dobbed them in' over the banner, but was there something that Tedesco and Davey could do to pre-empt that and get to the nub of the issue more quickly?

Lynne readily agreed to her partner's suggestion of a drink after work. They hadn't done this for a while, despite the fact that discussing things out of the office had often paid dividends in the past.

So, at 6.30 that evening they found themselves in the familiar setting of the Kingfisher, overlooking the River Rhyme.

Tedesco just beat his colleague to it and had already ordered their usual – a white wine spritzer for her and a large glass of Bordeaux for him – when he saw her arriving.

He felt the familiar frisson that always ran through him when he saw Lynne outside the workplace. She looked more attractive than ever tonight, he thought. She had a new electric blue jacket and he jealously wondered whether Duncan had helped her choose it, maybe on one of their outings to Bristol.

Their discussion did prove fruitful. "Lynne, I think I am having a lightbulb moment, or it may be the wine talking."

"Look, if you have invited me here to try and persuade me to stay…"

"No, no, of course not. I'm very happy for you both. It was about Sean and Jayne. I wonder if anyone has asked the gift shop at Rievaulx about who bought the stencils. They were made especially for them, remember."

"They could have sold them online, I suppose," Lynne replied, "but do English Heritage gift shops sell their tat over the web?"

"Hmm. I've never thought about it, but surely most of the stuff they sell will be impulse purchases."

"I agree. If you were visiting Stonehenge, for example, would you order a plastic model of it before you went? Of course not. Look, John, Sally and I can hold the fort for a day or two. Why don't you get an invitation up to Helmsley? I am sure that Bob and Hilary would love to see you – especially if you bring Barker."

FORTY

Bishop Bob was delighted to hear from his old friend, but somewhat surprised at the urgency of the proposed visit.

"It's about your successor, Bob. I'm looking into it with the approval of the police."

"I'm not surprised – you know more about what makes Rhyme tick than anyone else – and it was you who got them to reopen the case of poor Kerry Franklin."

Tedesco and Davey had been instrumental in the eventual, somewhat reluctant decision of Area Commander Hinton to investigate the case of the unfortunate volunteer who fell from the cathedral tower in suspicious circumstances.

While Tedesco prepared to travel north, the police had quickly tracked down Sean and Jayne, who were living in a shared house off South Western Way, the somewhat scuzzy approach to the railway station.

They both readily admitted to working on the 'Aelred' banners, but denied any role in forcing Silas to cut out the symbol. They were told not to venture too far from Rhyminster for the next few days, as there may be further questions.

DC Matt Lovell and DS Julia Tagg, who had been seconded to assist the Avon and Somerset force, were less than convinced by the denial. Why would Silas make this up?

*

Meanwhile, at the offices of Tedesco and Davey in Minster Precincts, Lynne was experiencing her own lightbulb moment.

As John was leaving for Helmsley in two days' time, she had negotiated a day's leave for the following day to have a look around Bristol and register with some estate agents there.

She called the deanery, hoping to speak to her friend Jo, the dean's wife and acting PA.

"Hi, Lynne. This is a surprise. I was going to call you for a catch-up. Fancy a coffee or whatever in the refectory?"

Having cheerfully agreed to meet Jo at 11.30, Lynne had a couple of hours to catch up on some executive recruitment work and to listen to Sally bang on about solar panels.

"Look, Sally, John and I are hardly climate change deniers, but it isn't exactly straightforward with a building like this – and we are both incredibly busy."

Not too busy for both of you to swan off at a moment's notice, Sally thought, wisely opting to keep silent.

Entering the always busy refectory, Lynne scanned the crowded tables for signs of Jo.

She was suddenly aware of an urgent presence at her side.

"Sorry, sorry. Running late. Long call from Judy at the Friends Office – she wanted ideas for a speaker at their annual do. I don't suppose you or John would be interested?"

"We are both pretty committed for the foreseeable – but why not ask DCI Bloomfield? He's always up for this sort of thing."

"But I thought he hated the cathedral? Anyway – lovely to see you."

Correctly taking this as her cue to explain the reason for her earlier call, Lynne said that she wondered whether Jo had an address for Bishop James' widow, Stephanie.

Jo was one of Lynne's best friends, so she had been told about the move to Bristol.

"I see. Are you looking for contacts for when you move up there?"

"Yes – she lives in Clifton, I think, so she might have some insights into what it's like to live there. Duncan and I are looking in the area – we think we could stretch to a bijou apartment once we've both sold up in Rhyme."

Jo, who knew her friend only too well, smiled.

"Okay, on that basis I will email you her details – but I am sure there is something detective related behind this."

"Jo, for a new age yoga person you are quite the cynic."

"And as a new age type, I fancy a green tea…"

*

Twenty-four hours or so later, Lynne was wandering around Clifton. Her lie, if not pure white, had been at least a bit smudgy. As she was in Bristol she did register with a few agents, but Duncan Chivers was nowhere to be seen and he was completely unaware of her visit.

Having located the exclusive mews where Stephanie Walker lived, and having used the previous afternoon to look into her lecture schedule, easily managing to lull her chatty PA into telling her that Ms Walker would probably be working from home in the morning, Lynne found a suitably convenient artisan coffee house, which offered excellent views of the lecturer's property.

She sipped her flat white slowly. It could be a long stake out.

However, after twenty minutes a leather-clad female emerged from the mews apartment. She stopped to shake down her hair, before gathering it together and pushing it under her helmet.

Lynne took pictures on her state-of-the-art phone, snapping away, convinced that this was indeed the grieving widow.

The woman then walked a few yards to where a black motorbike was parked in a residents-only bay and, with a certain flourish, she kick-started the machine and roared off towards the city centre.

It looked like Lynne's wild guess might have been right. She had been struck by the lack of any detailed description of the mystery courier who had delivered the suspicious package to the Soaked by the Spirit festival, but Tim Goodacre had informed the police that the rider had been 'slight' in appearance.

Could it actually have been a woman? And Stephanie Walker had always bothered her. By all accounts, she had been unemotional when her husband was killed. Different people react to death in different ways – but the dean had told Tedesco that Stephanie had appeared *glacial* when he visited her on the night of the murder.

Taken with her sighting of Walker and Neighbour together in the restaurant and the admittedly weird reference by the Raven to a beast from the ends of the earth, could there be an Australian connection that they had missed in their dogged pursuit of the Aelred theory?

FORTY-ONE

"Are you sure you can manage without me?"

This wasn't like him at all. Perhaps he was still struggling to get used to the concept of her not being around every day; he hated being separated from Barker, so was he transferring his separation anxiety to her?

Wisely, Lynne had kept quiet about her discovery in Bristol. She would pursue her own lines of enquiry, which may well get nowhere. It was more than possible that Stephanie could produce an alibi for the day of the Christian rave or whatever it was, and in the meantime, there would be the small matter of establishing that her bike was a match for the one seen roaring away from Charters Farm.

"Oh, I don't know. Sally, shall we try to persuade him to stay, as poor little defenceless women like us need our strong protector and his terrifying guard dog?"

At this, Barker appeared at Lynne's side, sidling up to her for a cuddle.

"Very funny. Okay, we will hit the road mid-morning if that's all right with you both."

"John?"

"Lynne?"

"You will call when you get there, let us know you arrived safely?"

"Hilarious."

*

Tedesco and Barker wandered back through the Close. As a well-trained pet, the border terrier performed his pre road trip ablutions, which meant that his master could break the back of the journey before needing to stop for a 'Penelope'.

The car had been packed on the previous evening and Tedesco had sorted out his playlist for the long journey ahead. Apart from the usual suspects – Clifford T Ward, Nick Drake, James Taylor – he'd chosen a selection of female voices from the 1980s, somewhat dangerously up to the minute by his standards.

As well as Beverley Craven and Julia Fordham, he had selected the first Fairground Attraction album, with lead vocals by Eddi Reader.

This trip was going to be 'Perfect'.

*

Once her partner had finally departed the office, Lynne made several attempts to get hold of her friend and one-time protégé DS Julia Tagg.

She got a call just before one.

"Lynne – I can give you five minutes."

Lynne used the time to run through her somewhat left-field theory about Stephanie Walker.

"As you know, Matt and I are helping the Somerset guys with the Rhyme end of things, but not sure this extends to checking speed cameras on their patch."

"Yeah, but think about it, Jools – if it was the lovely Steph then she may well have set off from Rhyminster: she was still living in the bishop's gaff, at least at weekends."

"And the festival was on a Saturday! Okay, leave it with me. Traffic have still got some active cameras between here and the county border."

Lynne forwarded her photos of Stephanie Walker and the motorbike to Jool's personal email.

*

After a break at Tedesco and Barker's now regular stop at the pub in the Derbyshire countryside, and despite a certain amount of M1 hassle, they arrived at Helmsley in good time for one of Hilary's legendary teas.

Two scones down, correctly served in the Devon style, the much more relaxed former bishop of Rhyminster, who presented as a living example of the benefits of retirement, suggested a wander down to the microbrewery before supper.

"Leave Barker with me," said Hilary. "He can help me with the prep, and we have a lot of catching up to do, don't we?" The latter comments were addressed to the terrier, who responded with a vigorous bout of tail wagging.

FORTY-TWO

It was market day in Rhyminster, and the square was buzzing. As well as Rhyme's notoriety as a crime scene there had been a more positive development in the city's recent history.

The past decade had witnessed a steady influx of well-to-do ageing hippies, by no means all from the UK, attracted by the ancient vibes and also by the ready availability of top-quality local produce that was evident from the abundance of overflowing fruit and vegetable stalls.

Somewhat predictably, Tedesco sneeringly referred to this group as the 'Back in the Day' brigade, but in some ways, he envied them. After all, some of his musical heroes from the past were, if not out-and-out hippies, certainly advocates of peace and love and wearing your hair long.

I cite in evidence the cases of Messrs James Taylor, Neil Young and Clifford T Ward, m'lud.

When he was at grammar school, Tedesco and his mates looked on with admiration at the long-haired students at the adjacent Plymouth Art College, even while they were shouting hilarious comments at them like "Hey, man, are you going to San Francisco?" from the safety of the school playground.

Back in the present, Sean Treagust and Jayne Rice-Foxton had concluded their weekly trip to the wholefood stall and were sharing a pot of artisan chai outside Pedro's, the go-to café for the alternative crowd.

Sean looked around somewhat shiftily, as if he was being watched or overheard.

"Look, I get it, but it wasn't me who intimidated that wally Silas, at least not directly."

Jayne looked at him with a mixture of contempt and exasperation.

"That's bullshit, Sean. You know it is. You told – more like ordered – poor old Silas to snip out that 'A' lettering. There was no one else involved."

"Listen. I said I wasn't directly responsible for this. Do you think I'd have been so heavy-handed if I hadn't had my arm twisted by that evil sod?"

"Okay, but by denying all to those detectives you've landed not just yourself in it but all of us. And you still haven't told me who forced you to do it. Was it the Raven?"

"I've got it covered. Aelred is my intercessor, and God is with us."

That evening, in the land of Aelred, Tedesco's route to the bar at the microbrewery had been interrupted by several regulars enquiring after Barker.

"Good to see you again, but where's Barker? He's a champion little pal, isn't he?"

As it was getting colder, he and Bishop Bob had retreated inside for their second pint of Yorkshire Legend.

During their al fresco first pint, Bob had gently enquired

after Tedesco's mental health. "I've heard about Lynne and Duncan. I know that you were never an item, exactly, but it must be difficult. Is she going to stay on at the agency?"

"Gosh, so the Rhyme rumour mill extends beyond the M1! Okay, I can tell you and Hilary. I was pretty devastated and took to wallowing in self-pity."

"I expect you have a playlist for that."

Tedesco laughed. "I do."

"Well, it's not the worst way of dealing with lost love."

"I'm not sure it was ever love exactly, but we were – are, I hope – close."

"Another one of your 'tendresses', Mr Registrar?"

"Maybe. But if Lynne is going to settle down, I'm glad it's with Duncan."

"I get that. He's one of the good guys. But what about the agency?"

"She thinks she can telecommute, if that's still what they call it. You know, work from home several days a week. It might be do-able for the executive recruitment stuff, but I need her with me on the ground – you literally have to sniff out the local clues in this business. You can't do that from Bristol."

Once Tedesco had returned with their second pint, his friend changed the subject.

"So, John. I think it's time you told me what this visit is really about."

"This is going to sound mad, but I – we, actually, as Lynne agrees with me – think that there may be a link between St Aelred of Hexham and the murder of your successor as Bishop of Rhyminster."

Bob took a deep breath. "I agree. It does sound mad, but your gut instincts are often spot on about these things. Try me."

Tedesco spent the next half an hour outlining the background to the Aelred theory, while the retired bishop listened intently.

"Okay, John. Two things. Firstly, we need to get back for supper. It's toad in the hole with a bottle of Jos' burgundy to keep it company. And secondly, I think you and I need to drive over to Rievaulx as soon as it opens to the public in the morning."

FORTY-THREE

A combination of bad weather, eagerness to get to Rievaulx as soon as it opened and lingering over breakfast meant that there was to be no reprise of Tedesco's earlier pilgrimage to the Abbey on foot.

Barker, having taken one look at the rain, seemed more than happy to stay behind with Hilary.

Bob drove carefully through the misty Yorkshire morning but they still had five minutes to kill when they arrived at the Abbey at 9.55am.

"John, the more I think about it I cannot see Silas being any sort of suspect. He may be easily led but he is incapable of violence. I'm sure of it."

"I agree, Bob, but his prints do match the banners and, crucially, the letter 'A' that was removed."

"But from what you disclosed last night all that might prove is that he could have been responsible for putting the fragment in the package: it sounds unlikely that he would have taken a motorbike to the festival."

"Looks like movement," said Tedesco suddenly, noting lights visible in the reception area.

The two friends were, as intended, the first visitors of the day. Tedesco had intended to ask for the manager and then to employ his advocacy skills to try to persuade him or her to give them access to any CCTV coverage of the gift shop. Okay, they weren't police officers but the combined authority of a former ecclesiastical lawyer with the equivalent status of a district judge and a recently retired bishop would surely carry enough weight to convince the most pedantic jobsworth to grant them access.

He needn't have worried. The employee who greeted them was the same woman who had shown him the stencils on his previous visit. Her name badge announced her as Avril.

"Avril, if I may, you won't remember me…"

"Let me stop you. I remember faces – and you had a very memorable request. You asked about the stencils with the medieval script."

"That's incredible."

"And you don't have to introduce your friend," Avril said, with a Yorkshire directness that Tedesco found a little unsettling.

"Everyone knows Bishop Bob. How can I help you both?"

Tedesco explained that he was a private detective and that was why he had asked about the stencils.

"I did wonder," said Avril.

"Anyway," Bob interjected, "John is helping the police down south on a rather delicate matter and, for reasons that we cannot disclose, the Aelred stencil has become a possible clue."

Tedesco continued. "You see, we need to know if anyone else might have asked about the stencils, or might have bought one. I have some photos on my mobile."

After faffing about with the phone, Bob having to remind him to look at the gallery feature, Tedesco was eventually able to show Avril the pictures of Sean and Jayne that Lynne had sent through to him.

"No, I don't recognise either of them.

"But don't look so sad," she went on, sensing the detective's disappointment, "I do remember the other person who asked about them. He was a huge chap. He bought several of them. I remember that – we had to reorder."

Bob glanced at Tedesco.

"Avril, is the coffee shop open?"

She indicated that it was.

"In that case, Bob and I will go and have a hot drink, warm ourselves up, and then we might need to see you again."

They both ordered cappuccinos as it seemed appropriate to the monastic surroundings.

Bob stirred in some sugar and then he asked Tedesco why he had suddenly suggested a coffee when they were still in mid-conversation with the helpful Avril.

"Fair point. Okay, another of our left-field possibilities. If the Aelred theory proves to be a blind alley we have another angle."

"I'm all ears."

"Australia. We have been looking at the chief executive of the diocese."

"Keith, the Neighbour from Hell, you mean. Although I'm up here, Rhyminster folk do keep in touch, so news of his reputation has spread beyond the Watford Gap."

"I'm not surprised. Look, when Avril said that the mystery stencil buyer was a huge chap I immediately thought of Keith. But I didn't have a photo of him to hand."

"So why don't we download one from the diocesan website?"

FORTY-FOUR

Lynne was rather enjoying minding the shop. Tedesco wasn't exactly a noisy colleague, but he did tend to interrupt her train of thought with his latest theories.

Jools had been in touch. Stephanie Walker's motorcycle had been confirmed as a Yamaha XSR 125 Legacy. This was a popular model, so there could be several visible on the traffic cameras. She would get back to her with any possible matches.

Meanwhile, DCIs Hill and Bloomfield were having an impromptu case conference over Microsoft Teams.

"So, Jimmy, where are we? Still nothing on the murder weapon, so what have we actually got? Tim Goodacre's revelation about the package delivered to the site. The gardener's prints all over the banners – but he claims to have been working at Derrington Hall, and Lady Fiona seems to be going out of her way to back him up – and now we have the two activists that Silas is trying to implicate."

"Do you want my team to have another word with them?"

"Good idea. They were pretty evasive, I gather, especially him. He denies bullying Silas into cutting out the symbol but seems to be hinting that he was pushed into getting the deed done by someone else."

"Or might it be a group? Tedesco and Davey have been looking into this cult of Aelred. It all sounded a bit crystals and dream catchers at first but they may be on to something."

"The LGBT angle? I can see how the late bishop would have inflamed that community with his views – and not just that community. The tolerant majority was pretty disgusted as well."

"But would these monk worshippers go so far as to kill someone, let alone a high-profile figure? Tedesco showed me some of this Aelred guy's greatest hits, as it were: it's all peace and love, man."

Back in the refectory at Rievaulx, the bishop had easily found Keith Neighbour's profile on the 'people' section of the diocesan website. In fact, Neighbour dominated it – it was as if a communist-era cult of personality had taken over the ancient see, with Neighbour cast as Enver Hoxha or Nicolae Ceausescu.

Poor Pete Leiper, the Bishop of Dartmoor, who was supposed to be in charge of the diocese, barely got a mention.

There was even a section headed 'Praise for Keith from the Parishes' where various local stalwarts posted glowing tributes to the Australian. Tedesco wondered aloud what funding for a new toilet, or urgent roof repairs, had been dangled before the parish officials in return for a glowing tribute.

"Look," said Bishop Bob, "before we show Keith Neighbour's bestial visage to Avril, why do you think it could be him, apart from her description of a huge man?"

Tedesco stroked his imaginary beard as if in two minds as to how far he should go.

"I have probably stretched your credulity enough for one day, Bob, but here goes. Wilf Drake told me about an unfortunate incident in the cloisters before the early Sunday service."

Bob poured another sachet of sugar into his coffee. "Go on."

"This is going to sound bonkers, but one of the volunteers was scared out of his wits by a guy dressed in black—"

Bob butted in. "Calling himself 'The Raven', perhaps?"

"You have heard of him!" spluttered Tedesco, almost spilling his coffee.

"Oh yes. And he is no conventional crank. The deliverance chaplain has a file on him. If he is involved then no, I don't think what you are about to tell me will be in any way crazy."

"Okay, so here goes.

"The police went to see the Raven. Wilf had asked around at the Street Pastors and one of them told them that he might be found at the Ring."

"I could have told you that, saved Wilf the effort. This man thinks he is the guardian of the site and he intimidates any visitors he doesn't like the look of with his horrible dog, Grebo."

"Who calls a dog Grebo?"

"Indeed. But, John – what has the Raven got to do with your Neighbour theory?"

"He told the young constables who saw him – and they were pretty traumatised by the experience – that he knew that there was a beast from the ends of the earth that was devouring its prey in the cathedral. Or at least that was the gist of it."

"So you thought ends of the earth, Australia, someone menacing the cathedral, Neighbour."

"Got it in one. Shall we go and find the lovely Avril?"

*

Bloomfield called in Lovell and Tagg. "I've been conferring with DCI Hill. We think we need to call young Sean Treagust in, ask him nicely to visit the station to help with some more enquiries."

"What about Jayne?"

"Let's leave her to stew. He is the one that Silas has accused of forcing him to tamper with the banner."

"I agree," said Julia Tagg. "And his denial was somewhat pathetic. We need to establish that he did meet Silas."

"And," Matt Lovell added, "if he is claiming that he too was forced into this in some way it would only be natural to ask who applied the pressure."

FORTY-FIVE

A healthy queue of visitors had built up at the reception desk, so Tedesco and Bob hovered about and examined some of the other Aelred-related merchandise while they waited for Avril to become free, Barker's master using the opportunity to buy his friend some Rievaulx Abbey dog treats. He was attracted by the image on the packet, which showed some medieval monks wandering around with what looked like a Yorkshire terrier. Sweet.

"So, gentlemen," said Avril. "You look like you want to ask me about the man I saw."

Tedesco was warming to Avril and her direct ways. What a refreshing contrast with his own ditsy PA, Sally.

Bob snatched Tedesco's phone, rather rudely for a man of the cloth, his friend thought, and showed her the picture of Neighbour.

There was no equivocation, no intake of breath or sucking through teeth with Avril.

"It's him. No doubt. No need to phone a friend. Final answer."

"I'm not going to the station to help them with their enquiries. They can go and do one."

"Very mature," said Jayne. "Look," she said more gently, "you aren't under arrest, you are going voluntarily. If you refuse, won't it look as if you have something to hide?"

Sean bit his fingernails. She was right – but he did have something, or more accurately someone, to conceal.

*

Nicola Tedesco had taken the morning off work to meet her solicitor, Susannah Shaldon, as there had been developments.

When Neil Sparkes had recommended his colleague to Tedesco at the Rhyminster FC match he'd described her as terrifying.

Nicky saw her as reassuring, someone you would want in your corner.

From a second-generation Caribbean background, she stood out in 'hideously white' Rhyme and Nicky wondered how she was finding it after practising in London.

"So, Nicky," the lawyer said, opening an expensive-looking leather-bound folder, which looked as if it had come from Smythson.

"I've spoken to the other side" – which was how she referred to Chag's solicitors – "and it looks as if we may have a temporary solution, which will at least keep you and Ella safe in Crane House for now."

"How so?"

"The bank are prepared to hold off taking any steps to enforce the charge on the property."

Nicky interrupted. "In lay language?"

Susannah laughed. "Sorry, and I should be more careful when my client is a famous journalist! It means that they won't call in the loan on the house. They won't sell it to pay the company's debts."

"So why the change of heart?"

"Firstly, the bank will have been advised by their own legal team that they are on a sticky wicket with you. They should have insisted that you were independently advised before you signed your share of the house over. Secondly, Chag seems to have accepted the reality of his position and is looking to either sell Aspirational Motors as a going concern or look at refinancing the company."

"Okay, so how long have we got?"

"They've given him six months to sort things out, then they will review the position again."

"Well, good news I suppose but I'm surprised that the bank is being so tolerant."

"They have got *some* money out of him. He's sold the Porsche and the boat."

"Ouch, he won't like that. Thanks, Susannah. I think I need to use the time to think about what I do if he can't sell up."

Although this all sounded positive, Nicky knew who she would want to discuss it with when he got back from Yorkshire.

Tedesco would be returning home the next day, but in the meantime Hilary was happy with his suggestion that she should join the rest of the household for a last drink at the microbrewery before the detective treated his friends to a fish supper from Deep Blue.

After a lovely evening, his last thoughts were of his late love Sorcha in West Cork and the mystery of the carving in the chapel of St Nonna. Just who did it remind him of, and did it have a bearing on the investigation? It was starting to really irritate him.

He used his internal soundtrack to finally coax him into a deep sleep.

It was the soothing, crystal-clear voice of Rumer: 'Where've You Been?'

FORTY-SIX

Jayne dropped him off outside the Bristol Road police station. Her trust fund ran to a VW Polo.

"Remember. You are going voluntarily. If they do arrest you, bell me, but they will only do it if you try and pull the wool over their eyes."

"Easy for you to say."

Matt Lovell greeted him at the desk. "Mr Treagust. Thank you for agreeing to come in at short notice. This way please – and would you like a tea or coffee?"

Once they reached the interview room it was clear that Jools Tagg was missing.

"Sorry about this, Sean – can I call you Sean? My colleague will be here soon. Now, can I get you that drink?"

"Only if you have green tea."

The reason for DS Tagg's atypical lateness was that she was still on the phone to Minster Precincts. There had been a sighting of a motorcycle on the day of the festival, and it matched the one that Lynne had seen in Bristol. The rider looked slightly built and it could have been a woman.

The driver had been careful to stick rigidly to the speed

limits as the bike powered along the A38.

"That's great, Jools, but do the plates match?"

"We will never know. The bike we found on the cameras had an obscured number plate."

"But isn't that still an offence?"

"It is, but practically impossible to enforce."

"Because you can't identify the owner?"

"Indeed. And we haven't exactly got the resource to send a car in hot pursuit."

"So, what next?"

"I'm going to have to tell Verena and Jimmy. Left to me I think we should pay Stephanie Walker a visit. We can ask her about the plates as any offence would have taken place on our patch, but she is high profile."

"And wealthy."

DS Tagg apologised for arriving late. "I'm sorry to have held you up, Sean. I had to conclude what I was doing. Anyway, this shouldn't take long. DC Lovell?"

Having been unsubtly cued in, Matt once again complimented Sean on his good citizenship, before asking him a direct question.

"When we left you the other day there seemed to be some doubt in your mind as to whether you were present when the protest banner was cut. So could you confirm if you were present?"

"I was," said Sean, speaking barely above a whisper, "but I didn't cut it out, it was Silas."

Jools cut in. "Yes, you told us that he carried out the excision. But thank you for clarifying that you were there. Matt?"

"Thank you, DS Tagg. Sean, can you explain why the centre of the banner was removed?"

Sean looked at the floor.

"Do you need a moment? This may be important."

The two detectives could almost feel the cogs whirring. As Jayne had advised him, Sean had a decision to make. Either tell the truth and risk upsetting Keith Neighbour or keep quiet to protect the intimidating chief executive.

Sean opted for the first option.

"Look, officers, I want to make a statement. And I could use a coffee – I really don't mind if it's instant."

"Well done, Sean," said Jools. "That can't have been easy."

*

After a bright and early start from Helmsley, Tedesco and Barker were back in the office by the early afternoon.

"Anything happened while we were away? Any more suspicious deaths in the cathedral for example?"

"Not even remotely funny," said Lynne. "But I need to tell you about Stephanie Walker."

"And I need to tell you about Keith Neighbour."

Tedesco listened somewhat restlessly to Lynne's account of her day off in Bristol.

"I am shocked, horrified even. You lied to me, Lynne."

"Only a bit. I did register with some agents. And you would have tried to put me off."

Tedesco sighed. "You are right, of course. Look, do you really have to move up there? Can't you go up at weekends? Have a two-centre relationship?"

"Like the bishop and his wife, you mean? That ended well!"

Her colleague put his hands up in mock surrender.

"Okay, so now I will tell you about Keith Neighbour."

When he had finished, Lynne took great pleasure in telling him that he had also been somewhat economical with the actualité, before making the practical suggestion, in part based on her disclosure to Jools, that they ought to be sharing their findings with DCI Hill.

The senior officers were moving in the same direction. Jools had gone to Bloomfield with Lynne's theory about Stephanie, for which she received a mild reprimand for involving the traffic division without talking to him first.

The DCI had seen Sean Treagust's statement, which had clearly identified Keith Neighbour as having bullied him into making Silas cut the 'A' from the banner.

Jools tried not to recoil as her superior officer made the incredibly irritating church-steeple gesture with his hands, a sure sign that he was thinking carefully about what to say next.

"We need to get the band together again or else we are all going off in different directions. We need DCI Hill, you and me, Tedesco and Davey. Talk to Lynne, see if you can get them on board, and I'll check when Verena has a gap in her dance card."

FORTY-SEVEN

Jayne was proud of Sean. It had taken guts to make the statement, but he was clearly terrified. What would Neighbour do when he found out that he had pointed the finger of blame at him?

The ever-practical Ms Rice-Foxton calmed him down.

"Look, the first that hideous man will hear about it is if and when the feds decide to interview him. And if they do he is hardly going to do you harm, as they will know straight away that it was him."

Her fellow campaigner smiled shyly. "You are right, of course. And I do feel proud. I couldn't bear to leave Silas in the frame, poor sod."

*

Tedesco had responded to his sister's urgent request, and he and Barker found themselves driving over to Woolford just as it was getting dark.

He had Don McLean's *American Pie* album lined up on the CD player and, once they were out of the commuter traffic, he selected 'Winterwood', just right for the mood and the season. Barker seemed to like it as well.

It was to be a supper à deux. Ella was at choir practice and Jack was away at 'uni' – how Tedesco hated that disgusting and debasing shortening of the perfectly good 'university'.

It was probably an Australian thing, a deleterious import from down under to rival that of the chief executive of Rhyminster diocese.

After he had recovered from Nicky's trademark effusive greeting, he and Barker made their way to the large leather sofa in the conservatory for pre-supper drinks.

Nicky produced the special dog bowl that was kept at Crane House for the terrier's royal visits, while John opted for a tonic water. As ever, his sister was on the white wine.

The local-TV legend got straight to the point.

After summarising the recent developments in the divorce negotiations, which Tedesco listened to with engaged interest, she set out her very real concern.

"Cards on the table. What if my lovely husband can't sell the business? I don't imagine that this is exactly boom time for luxury cars, at least not down here.

"And Rochelle – she's bleeding him dry."

After venting over her husband's new partner – the age gap, the lack of any obvious job, apart from some influencing on social media – Nicky was uncharacteristically catty as she referenced the rumour that Rochelle had unsuccessfully applied to be a contestant on *Love Island*.

"Finished?" her brother said. "Okay, let's look at this calmly. There must be a chance that Chag can sell the business. It never ceases to amaze me how the top end of the property market always seems so resilient – look at how prices surged down here during Covid. And I wouldn't be at all surprised if it wasn't the same for cars. Banks are pragmatic. They wouldn't grant him more time unless there was a decent chance that they could recover their losses from a sale."

Nicky visibly relaxed in her seat and stroked Barker.

"But what if I do lose the house? Would you take us in if we were desperate?"

"So, you'd have to be desperate to put up with us, would you? Barker and I are offended!

"But," he went on, "it won't come to that. Although the courts try and avoid issues of conduct I think that Chag's behaviour has been such a huge factor in the collapse of the marriage that they couldn't ignore it, if it got that far. But it won't. Who is Chag's solicitor?"

"Can't you guess? Flick Gallant."

The ice-cool Felicity had been a prominent player in Tedesco's last big case, that of the death of a volunteer who plunged from the cathedral tower.

"Sis, I'm not surprised. But Flick will read him the riot act on costs, and it sounds as if Susannah is more than a match for her."

"But can I rely on you if the worst happens?"

He took her hand and Barker, ever sensitive, moved towards her.

"You have always been able to rely on me. And Barker would love it if you and Ella moved in."

They retired to the kitchen for a simple but delicious supper, some kind of butternut squash based traybake.

"I thought you could do with a veg hit, bro."

"Perceptive as ever. My Yorkshire diet consisted of toad

in the hole and fish and chips. I had some beer though – that contains plenty of nutritious vegetable matter."

"So how were our lovely ex-bishop and Hilary?"

"In great form. Bob seemed several years younger."

"Sorry, John, I can't switch off from the day job. Why did you decide to go there out of the blue? Was it to do with Bob's successor?"

"I'm tempted to say 'no comment', but on a strictly Chatham House rules basis, the subject did come up."

"And how is the investigation going?"

"The police have some leads, but it's still a murky picture. Lynne and I have both come up with some left-field theories of our own, which is partly why I went up to Helmsley."

"Anything I can help you with?"

Tedesco helped himself to some more salad, then looked up at his sister.

"Maybe. Can you ask around the news desk to see if anyone has had any dealings with Keith Neighbour?"

*

While the Tedesco siblings were enjoying their supper at Woolford, Lynne was at her yoga class in Rhyminster. This took place in the deanery as the former music room had been converted into a studio by the dean's wife, Jo, a yoga and mindfulness teacher when she wasn't acting as her husband's PA.

Lynne's friend Julia Tagg was absent due to working late, probably on the Bishop Jim case, mused Davey.

But just as she was saying goodbye to the others at the door, Dean Dan suddenly emerged from his study.

"Lynne – I was hoping to catch you. Could you spare me a minute or two?"

She followed him back into his study. Although it was predictably booklined, the dean's broad cultural hinterland was more than hinted at by the presence of a large black and white photograph of the Beatles silhouetted against the early sixties Liverpool skyline.

"I don't want to delay your supper, Lynne, but is anything really happening with the investigation?"

Correctly sensing that she felt uncomfortable, he swiftly added that as she and John were working with the police, however informally, he understood that there were limits on how much she could share.

"But remember that I am an ordinary priest as well as a cathedral dean. The rules of the confessional apply just the same."

Lynne threw her head back and laughed. "You wouldn't want to hear my confessions, Dan. And we would be here all night!"

"Shall we change the subject?" said the Dean of Rhyminster, looking more than a little bashful.

Lynne nodded.

"Lady Fiona, Canon Wilfred, and I had a chat in private after Sunday Eucharist. Fiona told me that her gardener had been hauled in for questioning and had been scared out of his wits. They were cross-questioning him about Aelred of Hexham, I gather."

Lynne, back in ex-CID mode, established direct eye contact.

"I think 'hauled in' is more than a bit strong. He agreed to help with enquiries, like any good citizen. And I doubt if he was subjected to *Line of Duty* levels of interrogation. And you know about the Aelred link. We discussed it the last time I was in this study, and you referred me on to Henry Easton."

The dean looked up at her like a crestfallen schoolboy who had been told off by his favourite teacher.

"Of course, sorry. But do I take it that Silas is no longer a suspect? Fiona says that he is vulnerable."

"I'm not the police, let alone the Crown Prosecution Service, but I can say that other lines of enquiry are opening up."

"Good, good."

"Can I ask you something?" Lynne said.

"Of course."

"How is the diocese managing without the bishop? I understand that the chief executive is still very much in post."

Dean Dan rolled his eyes heavenwards. "He is. But to be fair, which isn't easy where he is concerned, our good Neighbour is keeping us afloat. I gather that the finances have been stabilised and poor old Bishop Pete leans on him to the extent that some are even referring to 'Bishop Keith' as the real power in the land."

"That's kind of what John and I had been picking up. Look, could you – and Fiona and Wilf – keep an eye on him and let us know if Neighbour does, or says, anything of note?"

"Yes, of course. Do you think he might be involved?"

"Nice try, Mr Dean. Just keep an eye on him, that's all we are asking."

FORTY-EIGHT

When he got back from Woolford, Tedesco felt surprisingly awake, and so he located his latest casebook, this one headed 'The Case of the Turbulent Bishop'.

As we have seen, he always wrote up his notes by hand, using his favourite ink pen. He found that this aided concentration, and he also relished the opportunity it gave him to exercise his skill. He wrote in beautiful copperplate.

He needed to order his thoughts more precisely before the meeting with the police, so he prepared to summarise them.

"Perhaps," he pondered aloud, "had I been a monk in medieval Rievaulx, could I have found work as a scribe for Aelred?"

Carefully turning down the next blank page in his light blue counsel's notebook, he began to write, starting with the background to the murder.

First of all, we have the controversial appointment of the bishop followed by the 'medieval flummery' sermon, which sparked the idiotic walkout by the

Master of Musick. Then there were the comments about minorities, which triggered the much more dignified protest from Jos Elsted and his friends.

This was followed in short order by the Rhyme equivalent of Robespierre's Terror as the bishop and his henchman imposed their zealotry on the diocese.

Next up, Bishop Jim was found head down in a yurt in Somerset on the very day that I attended the meeting in the Safe House, which the dean had called in order to brainstorm how we might rid ourselves of the man who Canon Wilf referred to as our turbulent bishop.

Then the reports came in of the mysterious lettering found on the bishop's body, and the motorcycle being seen zooming off into the distance while Keith Neighbour was dancing to the worship band.

His concentration was shattered by the sound of his phone, the jaunty tones of the Sousa march setting off Barker.

"It's only the phone! I know you hate it, old pal, but it needs to be loud so I can hear it! Tedesco! Who is this?"

"Hmm, maybe some work on the phone manner is called for. There are courses you can go on…"

"Oh, very funny, Lynne. You have just interrupted me mid-inscription."

"Is that what you call it?"

"What? Oh, hilarious, police canteen humour at its best. Look, this had better be important."

"I thought you might be interested to know that I had a chat to our lovely Dean Dan this evening. He, Fiona, and Canon Wilf seem to have formed a kind of verbal WhatsApp group – anyway, I have asked them to keep an eye on Keith for us."

"Good move, but hardly worth a call."

"Maybe not. But I have also just heard from Jools. She had to miss yoga as she was working late."

"On this, I assume."

"Yeah. And the exciting news is that the boffins in CID have blown up the image of the motorcycle on the enforcement cameras and compared it with my shots of Stephanie Walker."

"Okay, but how would that help? Didn't you mention that the number plates were obscured?"

"I did. But the helmets matched. Stephanie and the mystery rider both wore helmets with a small but distinctive logo, which has been tracked down to an Australian brand… it features a tiny kangaroo."

Tedesco took a few seconds to process this. "So, I guess that Ms Walker will be getting a visit soon. Great work from you both!"

Lynne smiled to herself.

"See you tomorrow, you patronising git. Get back to the inscribing or whatever unspeakable thing you are doing!"

Her partner ended the call. He wanted to finish his summary that night and now he could update it with Lynne's revelations.

But first he needed to regain his focus, so he went to his vinyl collection and pulled out his favourite James Taylor album: *Mud Slide Slim and the Blue Horizon*.

Helping himself to a glass of Jos Elsted's latest discovery from the Garonne, he used the tried and tested combination of music and wine to bring himself back into the zone.

FORTY-NINE

As the record ended with the lovely and incredibly apt 'Isn't It Nice to Be Home Again', Tedesco paused to consider the fate of the pop or rock album as a concept.

He regarded the best of them as works of art, up there with any painting or sculpture, which had to be listened to in full to appreciate the narrative arc of the artist. Did anyone under sixty spend evenings curled up with a favourite album anymore?

His thoughts then flew to the practical and once he'd settled Barker down for the night, he recommended work on his casebook.

Lynne researched the backgrounds of Neighbour and the bishop's wife. Apart from some salacious gossip linking them, she found that Neighbour owed his career to Stephanie's father. Was there something sinister going on? Were Ocker Walker, Stephanie and Neighbour conspiring to infiltrate the Church of England? And to what end? It was hardly a major force these days.

Thanks to Andrea at the cathedral shop and latterly Avril at Rievaulx Abbey, a clear link between the cult of Aelred and the murder of the bishop has been established.

And soon we discover that Silas cut out the 'A' symbol from one of the banners from the vigil. He tries to blame this on Sean for forcing him to do it.

Then the real developments. Firstly, Tim Goodacre wanders into the picture – shades of Jackson Browne: 'The Pretender'.

His production of the envelope that had been couriered to the festival and its contents doesn't completely exonerate Silas, but it raises questions about the significance of the leather-clad messenger. And it cements the centrality of Aelred to the case.

The Raven. At first I thought this was an entertaining sideshow, but based on what Bishop Bob and others have said, his hints about Neighbour as the beast from down under or whatever may have been prescient. Hope that Dan and Co. and maybe Nicky and the Searchlight newsroom can come up with more evidence of the chief executive's recent behaviour.

Lynne's discovery that Stephanie Walker is a most unlikely biker taken together with Avril's swift recognition of Neighbour's photo may be the big game changers we have been praying for – especially now we know that Stephanie's helmet matches the one on the speed camera.

But we still have no news on the murder weapon – and what about motive? Would followers of a gentle medieval saint be sufficiently livid at his message being

*betrayed by the modern church to cold-bloodedly kill
a bishop?*

*And what motive would Neighbour – or Stephanie
even – have for this gruesome attack?*

Unless it was the oldest motive in the world…

*And what about that carving in St Nonna's chapel?
It must have some bearing.*

After he decided to call it a day, Tedesco's sleep was
disturbed by visions of the face in the carving. Why couldn't
he work out the significance of it? Perhaps he needed to go
back to the chapel and take another look.

FIFTY

DCI Verena Hill and DC Kyle Brooks of the Avon and Somerset constabulary presented their warrant cards to the receptionist at the Faculty of Philosophy, then asked to see Senior Lecturer Stephanie Walker, only to be told that she was in the middle of a seminar.

"And when will she be free?" asked Hill.

"In about half an hour, at least. Why don't I tell her you called and then you can arrange a time?"

"No thank you. We will wait."

"Well, it's up to you, of course," said the receptionist – whose name badge revealed her to be Carole – with an insouciance that suggested an unfamiliarity with the concept of customer service.

DC Brooks was about to say something when his senior colleague stepped in.

"Why don't we go and get a coffee, DC Brooks?"

Carole, unhelpfulness personified, suggested the student common room, "but it might not be open".

"Bloody hell," said the young detective, "rude or what?"

The common room was empty apart from a couple of

students who cheerfully showed them how to work the coffee machine, before continuing what was clearly a gossip session rather than any musing on philosophy.

DCI Hill listened in, but none of the chatter seemed to involve Stephanie Walker, so after fifteen minutes or so they made their way back to the faculty office.

Down in Rhyminster Sally Munks had taken another call from Lady Derrington, an event that clearly made her day.

"Sorry about Sally, Fiona," said Lynne. "She gets a little overexcited when you call."

"I'm sure she's frightfully good. Anyway, the dean has asked me to report to you and John if I hear anything about the appalling Mr Neighbour."

Lynne grabbed a notebook and biro. "I am all ears."

"It probably isn't anything, but we had the parish AGM the other evening. It normally follows the same pattern every year, nothing much happens, quite dull really."

"So, what was different about this year? A falling out over the coffee rota?"

"A bit more than that. It was a first. Normally the accounts are nodded through, no questions from the floor. This time, after Fred Pound, the treasurer you know, a real sweetheart, asked for a proposer and seconder for his motion to accept the accounts, one of our newer members put his hand up."

"To propose the motion?"

"No, this new chap, Simon Hedley, funny little man, works in computers I think, asked about one of the entries in the accounts."

"Fiona, I can't stand the suspense!"

"I'm coming to it. There was a larger than usual payment to the diocese. As John will explain to you, the parishes all pay into a central fund to cover the priests' salaries and so on.

"Anyway, when poor old Fred went over the figures again, he had to agree.

"It turns out that hidden away in the usual bill we get from head office – Church House – was a reference to a special administrative charge. Fred promised to look into it, but before he contacted the diocese he put the word around with the other parish treasurers."

"I see. And did the other parishes receive similar invoices?"

"They did. And they have asked me to raise this anomaly with Church House as their unofficial spokesperson."

Lynne considered what she had been told, and then she resumed the conversation.

"I think I follow now. You think Neighbour might be behind this. Do you suspect that he might be diverting funds for his own benefit?"

"I have nothing to go on yet but think about our Antipodean friend. He has managed to insert himself into a trusting but somewhat outdated structure."

"And," Lynne added, "he has carved out a unique and seemingly unaccountable role, first as the bishop's fixer and now as chief executive. Fiona, this may be important, so please keep me in the picture."

"Of course. And, Lynne? I hope you will keep in touch when you move to Bristol. I do so enjoy our little chats."

Back in that booming city, the unhelpful Carole was in the midst of trying again to persuade DCI Hill and DC Brooks to come back another day, but she was thwarted in her mission by the sudden appearance of a human whirlwind who Hill instantly recognised.

"Dr Walker?"

The surprised lecturer spun round to face the CID officer.

"Yes. I'm very busy – can this wait?"

FIFTY-ONE

After Lynne put the phone down, she carefully considered what she had just been told by her favourite aristocrat.

This was something they should mention at their meeting with the police, surely?

She interrupted Tedesco, who was helping her on one of her corporate recruitment files, and pointed at the meeting room, asking Sally to get them some coffee.

"Was that Lady Fiona I heard you speaking to?"

"You know it was. She rang about the case. There could be a new angle. Neighbour may be ripping off the diocese."

Her partner did his annoying thing of standing up, looking out of the window at the view of the tower and then sitting down again.

"Hmm. Perhaps we should have thought of that. Look at the lovely Keith, the master of all he surveys. Who is really keeping an eye on him? With Bishop Jim's connivance, he abolished several of the committees that might have been expected to scrutinise his work and he frightened off long-standing stalwarts like Giles, who would have spotted any dodgy moves a mile off."

Giles Varcoe was a local accountant who had served the church for many years, and had acted as auditor for several local charities.

"And," continued Tedesco, "I gather from Canon Wilf that the finance committee has been watered down and that it has delegated much of its oversight function to a much smaller group."

"And I wonder who that consists of?"

"Keith, the bishop's widow and a tame accountant from outside the diocese, according to Wilf.

"The more I think of it," he went on, "the worse it could be. If Neighbour was given carte blanche to run things, he would have the power to distribute funds, benefit favoured clergy and their parishes, even make fraudulent grant applications."

"Easy tiger," said Lynne. "I agree with you. Neighbour probably has questions to answer about his handling of the finances.

"But," she continued, "that doesn't make him a murderer, does it?"

*

"No, I am afraid that this cannot wait, madam," said DCI Verena Hill, not someone who was in imminent need of assertiveness training.

"Is there somewhere private—"

"My office. Follow me. Carole, no interruptions please."

She led the two officers down a narrow corridor, at the end of which was a door bearing her name – 'Dr Stephanie Walker'.

As they entered a surprisingly spacious room with views of the Downs, Hill wondered how the bishop's widow, who was a relatively junior academic, had managed to snaffle what seemed to be the pick of the offices.

After gesturing Hill and Brooks to sit down, Dr Walker sat behind her expensive-looking partners' desk and fixed the DCI with an icy stare.

"Carole has explained who you are. Do I assume that this is about my late husband?"

DC Brooks started to offer condolences, but was cut short by the bishop's widow.

"So, where have you got to? Have you arrested those LGBT rights vigilantes yet?"

DCI Hill bit her tongue, while her colleague idly mused as to who would win a fight between these two strong characters.

"Dr Walker, the investigation is continuing at pace, but I am not at liberty to discuss operational matters with you as you will appreciate."

"Okay, so why are you here? I have a busy schedule, so will you get to the point?"

"Very well. Do you have a motorcycle?"

"What the hell are you asking that for? Yes, but Carole could have told you that."

"Dr Walker," said Hill, returning the icy stare, "in that case we would like you to accompany us to the station to further assist us with our enquiries. If you are not too busy, that is…"

As the academic somewhat truculently followed them to the car park, Hill winked at her junior colleague.

They had a game plan. They didn't have anything like

enough to justify charges in connection with the bishop's ghastly exit, but if Walker identified the bike, they could arrest her on suspicion of concealing the number plates. And then they would be in business.

The Raven

Colin Scopes, the longest serving of the cathedral's team of vergers, was about to lock up for the night.

As he checked to make sure that the building was empty – there had been incidents of homeless people trying to bed down for the night on the unforgiving stone floor of the cloisters – the timid verger became aware of what he would later describe as a sinister presence.

"Don't worry, Colin, I am leaving once we have spoken. I have been waiting for you."

Poor Colin, who had been traumatised by his unwitting involvement in the murder of the bishop's lay assistant a few years ago, froze on the spot.

"A warning, Colin. A warning to those who minister in this place."

As the figure came closer, the verger could feel his breath on him.

He also became fixated on a large ring on the man's index finger.

"Tell them that the Raven has spoken. And death is coming."

The figure seemed to disappear into the foggy night. There was no sign of him when Colin, his hands shaking, struggled to lock the main entrance into the great edifice.

FIFTY-TWO

It was the morning of the meeting with the police, which was being held in the conference room at Minster Precincts again as this was not a formal gathering that could take place at a police station.

Sally had arranged for some extra chairs to be borrowed from one of the neighbouring offices, causing Tedesco to wonder whether this was going to be like a family Christmas with relatives perched on uncomfortable garden furniture. Perhaps they could arrange for Bloomfield to have the duff seat?

He had already decided to begin his day with the early morning service at the cathedral. As well as the need for some quiet time to think before the meeting, he wanted to see that carving in the chapel again.

He and Barker snuck in to the Lady Chapel with two minutes to spare.

The service was being conducted by his friend Canon Wilfred Drake, and the kindly precentor smiled at him as he was formally led into the chapel, the oldest part of the medieval building, by the head verger, Izzie.

As she was holding the verge, the symbolic staff of the office holder, Tedesco remembered how a similar one had been used as a murder weapon in his first cathedral murder case.

His mind began to wander during the lengthy reading of the first lesson, reliving the call he had received from his sister on the previous evening.

Nicky had reminded him that he had requested her to ask around the news desk for any rumours or incidents concerning Keith Neighbour.

What she had uncovered didn't directly relate to Neighbour, but she thought it might be useful background.

There were persistent stories in circulation linking Stephanie Walker's father, media magnate Ocker Walker, with a takeover of *Searchlight*'s commercial rival Focus South West.

After reminding himself of his theory that Walker was using his daughter and his former henchman to infiltrate the Church of England with a view to making it an outlier for his right-wing evangelical agenda, he wondered why the mogul would be interested in a tiny commercial station based in Derry's Cross, Plymouth?

Was he trying to buy up the entire region?

As the precentor asked the little congregation to join him in prayer, Tedesco silently threw in one of his own.

Dear Lord, if you are there, please look after our special part of your creation.

Barker was looking very serious – he was probably joining in as well.

Tedesco's silent musings ended when he realised that the service had finished and, as he made his way to the exit,

Canon Wilf greeted him warmly and asked if he could spare him a moment.

"Yes, of course, Wilf. Barker and I are heading off to St Nonna. There's something I want to check in there."

"Okay, I'll see you once I've done the pastoral bit."

'The pastoral bit' referred to the routine greeting of the congregants as they left the chapel. For some of them, it would be the only conversation they would have that day; for others it was a chance to share a confidence, or admit to a worry.

In Tedesco's view Wilf excelled at the pastoral bit – he was up there with Trollope's sainted clergyman, Septimus Harding.

While he awaited the precentor, Tedesco made the most of his opportunity to reinspect the carved head in the little chapel dedicated to Nonna, the mother of St David, who was one of many Celtic missionaries who passed through the deep south-west on their way to Europe in the 6th and 7th centuries.

As he peered anew at the carving of the friendly-looking face, Tedesco wondered if it had anything to do with the investigation at all. Perhaps it was just someone he knew socially, his former colleague Neil Sparkes perhaps?

After all, the face depicted in the chapel looked like it was of someone who enjoyed the odd drink. This was really infuriating. Who did it really remind him of?

"Sorry to keep you, John," said the precentor, looking a bit flustered as he joined Tedesco and Barker.

"That's okay, Wilf. I've been looking at this carving," said the detective, pointing out the head carved into the screen.

"It's bugging me – it reminds me of someone."

The precentor smiled. "I can see who it is – it's Jos Elsted, isn't it?"

*

As the two friends continued their conversation, Sally and Lynne had in the meantime arrived at the office, Lynne's attempts to prepare for the important meeting being slightly thwarted by the PA's constant prattling about the recent visit of her beloved nephew Theo – or 'Theo the Thug', as Tedesco had somewhat unfairly christened him.

"Theo has some really good ideas about how we can modernise the agency – we have no presence on social media. The website is a start, but what about Facebook or Twitter? And Theo says that we should be on TikTok. It's the only way to connect with the young."

Lynne groaned. "Look, Sally, I know you mean well, but this isn't the time. And young people aren't really our key demographic."

"But they could be one day. Theo thinks you and Mr T could do a TikTok video."

"I think not. I can't see John rapping, can you?"

"Why not?" said Sally, before starting to rap herself, after a fashion.

"*We are John Tedesco and Lynne Dav-ee, the dope guys from the agen-cee.*"

Lynne retreated into the sanctuary of the interview room and screamed.

*

Back in the chapel, Tedesco had to agree with his friend.

"Of course, it's dear old Jos. You've solved the puzzle, Wilf."

The precentor smiled, then commented that he might have something to assist with the real mystery.

"Colin came to see me last night. He was locking up in the cloisters when he was approached by a stranger."

"The Raven strikes again?"

"Yes, I'm afraid so. And poor Colin is the last person I would want to be exposed to that terrifying creature."

"Agreed. So did the Raven make one of his portentous predictions?"

Canon Wilf nodded his head with weary solemnity.

"He did. He told Colin that death was coming…"

FIFTY-THREE

"Sorry we're late," said John, Lynne replying that he had better not blame his companion: "You are always punctual, aren't you?" she said to Barker, stroking the terrier under his chin.

The police were due in an hour's time, which the two friends and colleagues used to prepare for the meeting, Tedesco updating Lynne on that morning's news of the Raven and Nicky's story about the rumoured Aussie takeover at Focus South West, Lynne opting to leave any speculation about the Raven's latest prophecy until they had shared it with DCI Hill and her entourage.

The clapped-out old buzzer did its job in sending Sally hurtling down the winding staircase, a health and safety nightmare, but she somehow arrived safely at the bottom to greet their guests.

After Sally had concluded her fussy ushering of DCIs Bloomfield and Hill and DS Julia Tagg into the conference room and then taking an age over the coffee orders, Tedesco welcomed them more formally.

Although this was a strictly off-the-record gathering,

Verena Hill effectively took the chair – *fair enough*, thought Lynne, as the murder had been committed on her patch.

"I will start with some hot news. I called on Stephanie Walker yesterday, and she agreed to come to the station for questioning."

"About the motorbike?" asked Lynne.

"Yeah. And we have charged her for failing to display a number plate."

"Did she want a solicitor?" Tedesco asked.

"Oh yes. She wouldn't accept the duty guy and wouldn't talk until she had spoken to her own brief."

"So I assume she's on police bail?"

Hill nodded, and then conceded the floor to Tedesco, who was champing at the bit to share his latest news about the Raven. But as soon as he had got to the part about the latest prophecy, Bloomfield butted in.

"Just so you two know," he said, addressing his comments to the civilian detectives, "I have already explained about this nutcase to Verena. You don't really think this has any relevance to the price of fish, let alone this investigation, do you?"

Lynne snapped back at her former CID boss.

"It was the nutcase who focused our minds on Mr Neighbour, and let's not forget that he managed to traumatise two of Devon and Cornwall's finest when they tracked him down on Rhyminster Ring. So I think we do have to consider who might be in danger."

Bloomfield sneered. "What are you saying? We have a serial killer out there bumping off bishops? Who's next? Bath and Wells? The archbishop of Canterbury?"

Verena Hill intervened. "Look, Jimmy, I know this Raven guy sounds off the scale but irrespective of his soothsaying,

Lynne is right. There could be others who are caught up in this who might be in danger."

"Absolutely," said Tedesco. "Whoever has done this will be looking for people to blame."

Lynne nodded in support. "Silas, Sean and Jayne…"

Bloomfield took off his John Lennon style granny glasses and gave them a very deliberate polish with his pocket handkerchief.

"Okay, fair point. So do I call out a search party for Mr Raven and see if he can be more specific?"

"He won't be," said Tedesco. "His sort only deal in sweeping predictions. And the uniforms were lucky. He won't be so easy to track down a second time. He will have gone to ground somewhere else by now."

"In a crop circle near a ley line, I suppose."

Hill glared at her fellow DCI.

"John. What else have you and Lynne got?"

Tedesco had his case book open and took the rest of them through it carefully.

"An excellent – and if I might add, beautifully written – summary John."

"So where are we?" she asked rhetorically. "I am confident that we can link Ms Walker to the getaway bike, but that doesn't actually prove that she was the one driving it on the day."

"But if the helmets match, ma'am," said Julia Tagg, "who else could it have been?"

Hill thought carefully before replying. "I think we need to see Tim Goodacre again – the young man who brought the Aelred symbol in to show us."

"To see if he can recognise – I don't know – a physical similarity with Stephanie?"

"Or perhaps he could remember her voice, she must have said something when the package was handed over?"

"And shouldn't we at least get a statement from the woman in Yorkshire who says she saw Neighbour up there?"

"Haven't we arranged that yet? Get on to the local boys and get it done."

Lynne interjected between the officers.

"Look, I actually saw Stephanie Walker put her helmet on and drive the bike away when I was house hunting in Bristol, remember. So I think that does more than link her to the machine."

Hill shrugged, then gestured for Lynne to carry on.

"But at worst, I accept that Stephanie was only the decoy rider, so who actually killed the bishop?"

Bloomfield gave a knowing look at his fellow DCI, who stood up for extra effect.

"Okay, there has been a possible development. And this really is incredibly confidential. Jimmy and I weren't sure if we could mention it."

Bloomfield nodded as if to grant his permission to reveal.

Hill resumed. "The post mortem results disclosed significant traces of a poisonous substance which had been ingested by the deceased. Atropa belladonna."

Tedesco let out a sigh. "Deadly nightshade."

FIFTY-FOUR

Yvette Durand wasn't taking any chances. She had to be at the local airport by seven the next morning, so she luxuriated in a long bath, drank a mug of cocoa, took a couple of sleeping pills and had an early night. The taxi was due at five thirty and she had set her phone alarm for half an hour earlier.

She prayed that there would be no interruption from her neighbour upstairs.

They got on well – Stephanie lectured at the university, and they shared a love of art – but whenever her Australian boyfriend paid Steph a visit the sparks flew and the noise travelled.

This was one night when Yvette needed her beauty sleep.

*

The plan worked. The Cathedral School minibus was to be found in its usual place in the large car park area and he, as a school governor, had access to the entry code for the site, so he could enter after school hours.

Getting hold of the spare ignition key was a piece of cake. The headmaster's secretary had been all too easy to distract.

Silently congratulating himself for having persuaded the governing body not to install CCTV on costs grounds, he checked that no one else was in the vicinity and then gingerly drove out of the school gates.

FIFTY-FIVE

"Have we wandered into an Agatha Christie plot here?" said Lynne. "Is deadly nightshade even a thing?"

Hill patiently explained that the plant could be found in this country, that the berries were particularly dangerous to children and to adults if eaten in sufficient quantity.

"But the toxicology report showed that the root, which is the most poisonous element, had been ingested by the bishop. It looks like it had been ground into a powder and mixed with other stuff," Bloomfield said, with minimal attempt at detail.

Julia Tagg, who had been fairly quiet up until now, made a significant intervention.

"But surely the bishop was killed with a knife and then that gruesome lettering was applied to his back. Is there another theory, that he was killed by the plant?"

Sensing that Tedesco was about to speak, Verena Hill addressed the point.

"It seems unlikely, DS Tagg. My sense is that the poor man was poisoned prior to his ordeal."

"I agree," said Bloomfield. "The boffins think that the poison might have been administered earlier that morning:

it may have been mixed into a hot drink."

"Who could have done that?" Lynne speculated. "Mrs Bishop slipped it into his morning cuppa, do you think? Wouldn't he have tasted it?"

Tedesco spoke. "I have it on pretty good authority that the late bishop only drank some kind of herbal tea. It was on offer after his enthronement. Everyone who sampled it said that it tasted vile."

"So he may not have noticed if it had been spiked, then," said Lynne, before asking if anyone knew what the effect of drinking the poison might have been.

"It could have caused him to have blurred vision, drowsiness," said Bloomfield.

Tagg politely interrupted her boss.

"So he could have been alive but out of it when he got to the Christian rave?"

"Rather graphically put, DS Tagg," said Verena Hill, "but that's my assumption. He was, as you say, 'out of it', which might explain why there were no signs of a struggle when he was attacked."

"But, ma'am, can we assume that Stephanie Walker was the poisoner? Why would she do it?"

"Forced by Neighbour?" Tedesco offered.

"Jimmy has another theory."

Bloomfield fiddled with his bow tie and then pronounced, "The alternative crowd in Rhyme use all kinds of herbal remedies, so we did some digging and guess who was investigated for running a boutique cannabis farm? Our friend Sean."

After the meeting broke up, Tedesco and Davey reviewed progress.

There were several actors in the drama who had questions to answer. Stephanie was under investigation already – what was she doing on the day of the murder? Was she the mysterious courier? Had she poisoned her husband?

Or had Sean done so, or provided her with the means?

But what was there to link Sean the Aelred disciple with the hard-line evangelical lecturer with a taste for the writings of Ayn Rand, the heroine of the new right in western politics? Seems unlikely, surely?

And how about Keith Neighbour? Not only had he driven the bishop down to Somerset on the fateful day but Silas had all but accused the Australian of forcing him to cut out the 'A' from the banner.

And if Avril was to be believed, and Tedesco did, Neighbour had travelled all the way to Rievaulx to get hold of the Aelred stencils.

But hadn't he been filmed joining in with the crowd singing along to the worship band, which he would rely upon as his alibi?

"We didn't mention the stories about Neighbour's financial moves," said Lynne.

"Deliberately. We have nothing concrete to go on. We should see what Fiona can dig up at Church House before we involve our friends in the force. But if he was plundering the coffers, and the bishop had begun to have his own suspicions, then this would give him a motive."

"Granted, but why would Stephanie want to help Keith unless she was still fixated on him – remember those old photos in Australia?"

"Good point. But would she want her own husband

dead? Or maybe Neighbour saw the chance to get it together with his old flame and inherit some of Ocker's millions?"

As the tower clock struck one, Tedesco realised that he would be late for his daily visit to Joan at the bakery, so he summoned Barker.

Before they ventured out he asked Lynne to check in with Lady Fiona and see if she had got anywhere. If there was a suspiciously large hole in the church finances then this needed to be investigated urgently, whether it had any connection to the bishop or not.

*

The following morning, Jos Elsted, wine merchant and cathedral sidesman, was enjoying his routine early morning walk around the Close.

Since moving down from London he had become an early riser and his favourite time of day was the half hour between six thirty and seven when the Close was waking up.

As he wandered past the gates of the Cathedral School he noticed that the school's minibus was parked outside the gates. Upon closer inspection, he saw that the keys were still in the ignition. And someone was asleep on the back seats.

He knocked somewhat gingerly on the window, which woke the sleeper, who looked furious, giving Jos the 'V' sign.

The intrepid vintner was not easily deterred. He resumed his knocking, but as he was getting nowhere, he turned round and strode purposefully towards the school entrance.

Jos was a supplier of wine both to the school and its headmaster, his friend Geoffrey Latcham, and as a trusted tradesman he too was privy to the entry code.

The man in the minibus, seeing that Jos was opening the gates, leapt out of the vehicle and ran away towards the Chapter House.

Jos didn't see his face, but he had a pretty good idea who it was. How many other giants did he know in the Close?

His first thought was to report the matter to the headmaster, but then he decided that there was someone else who needed to know and in any case the head wouldn't be on duty yet.

As it was still a bit early to call Tedesco, Jos went back to his small but immaculately presented flat in the Close to complete his morning routine with breakfast and Radio 3.

FIFTY-SIX

Neighbour had timed his exit perfectly as the school was closed for the day, and evensong was still in progress.

The Close was deserted apart from some desultory foreign students who were wandering in the road. He glared at them with pantomime menace as he squeezed the vehicle through the Broad Street Gate.

What passed for Rhyme's rush hour was over, so he enjoyed a clear run to Bristol.

That call from Steph had really annoyed him. Good job he had no meetings in the parishes that night.

She was normally so calm under pressure, but all it took was for some local cops to put the wind up her.

His attempts to reassure her on the phone had failed, so here he was riding to the rescue.

The local Brit police were a bunch of lazy half-wits as far as he was concerned.

But Steph could still ruin everything if she spoke to them without a decent lawyer. Good job that he had access to Ocker's contact book.

He had remembered a sports centre car park within

jogging distance of her place so he found it quite easily without having to run the risk of using satnav.

Neighbour parked in a dark corner, under some trees, and made sure he had his kit bag with him. Depending on how things went, he might be spending the night.

He came fully prepared for anything – once a marine, always a marine.

*

As the Chief Financial Officer of Rhyminster Diocese had been another victim of Neighbour's putsch, the day-to-day finances of the unwieldy organisation were in the sole hands of Paul Twigger.

Paul had joined the staff at Church House from school and had just clocked up thirty years' service.

Although a more than competent bookkeeper, he had no experience of high-level oversight and his constant mantra was 'keep your head down and all will be fine'.

The poor chap had been losing sleep over the imminent visit of Lady Derrington, who had not been remotely satisfied with his initial response that all financial matters should be referred to Mr Neighbour.

"No, I need to see the person at Church House who deals with the parishes. Do you send out the invoices?"

Paul Twigger didn't stand a chance, and so he agreed to see Her Ladyship at the earliest opportunity – and he resolved not to mention her visit to his boss.

*

Neighbour had his own key, so he let himself into the apartment, where he found the bishop's widow on tenterhooks.

"What took you so long?"

"Look, sweetie, I had to move a shedload of meetings to get here. I came as soon as I was able. I could use a coffee – and none of that vegan crap."

As he made himself comfortable on the deep sofa, he heard the sound of Steph's expensive coffee machine percolating in the kitchen and, correctly sensing that this would be a slow process, he silently removed something from his kit bag and concealed it under a cushion.

"It was awful. They bundled me into a police car. What will the students think?" Stephanie said as she returned with the drinks.

"Did any of them see you?"

"No, but Carole did and she spoke to them. A DCI Hill and a DC Brooks."

Neighbour considered what he had been told. Carole the faculty secretary was a notorious gossip, a bitter woman who resented successful women like Stephanie Walker.

"When you sent out your distress call you mentioned that these two idiots were asking you about the bike," he said. "I hope you kept schtum until I fixed you up with a good brief."

"Of course I bloody did! I didn't arrive in Botany Bay on a convict ship! But they made it clear that they had an image of the bike speeding away from the festival. It was picked up heading towards Rhyminster with obscured plates."

"But they can't prove it was you, can they?"

"Because it wasn't me, was it? Why did you trust that useless Tim Goodacre?"

"Fair enough, he has some questions to answer, I grant you. But he came good when it mattered."

"But it gets worse, Keith. The police have pictures of me walking to where I'd parked the bike here, then riding it to the office."

"Oh Christ…"

"I hadn't finished! They have compared the helmet I was wearing with the one Tim had on him."

"And they are the same, we know that. But there was nothing on it which would make it easy to identify."

"Apart from the kangaroo logo."

"Jesus Christ, Steph. You could blow the whole story."

Stephanie Walker's public image was of someone who almost revelled in appearing cold and indifferent. Her reaction to what her lover had just said was one of pure Latin American fury as she turned around and slapped him hard across the face, drawing blood.

"Big mistake, Steph. I mean *big mistake.*"

"Why should I lie for you and end up in prison?"

"You are in this up to your neck, you scrawny little bitch."

"But I'm not a murderer!"

They stood facing each other like a couple of punch-drunk boxers for what seemed like several minutes until Neighbour broke the ice, coolly changing his approach – rather like a fund manager switching out of a poorly performing trust into something more promising.

He tilted his expression to one of concern and contrition. It usually worked.

"Listen, sweetie, this isn't getting us anywhere. I'm sorry. We need to stick together. I had come here to deal with the police for you – I've got the name of a top lawyer.

Can we start again? I don't know about you, but I could use a drink."

The bishop had banned alcohol from the North Canonry, but his widow had a plentiful supply from the Wine Society.

"Look," she said, "I'm still bloody furious with you, but I agree, I could do with a large glass of white. I'll open a bottle."

Neighbour followed her silently into the kitchen, having swiftly snapped on the pair of surgical gloves he had hidden in the sofa.

He waited until she bent down to remove the bottle of chilled Chablis from the wine cooler, then silently knelt down behind her and expertly placed his right arm around her neck, and then began to slowly strangle the life out of her as if he was a human boa constrictor.

As she fell to the floor he waited until all sign of life had been drained from his victim, then he carefully cleaned up after his handiwork.

Now it was time for the finale. He took a surgical mask and some other equipment from his kit bag, shook the canister and carefully peeled away enough of her blouse to allow him to find a sufficiently flat surface on her body.

He delicately placed the stencil on her back and, once he was satisfied, he applied the paint spray.

FIFTY-SEVEN

Tedesco woke with a start, convinced that this was going to be a challenging day and one where he would need to be at his desk in Minster Precincts in good time for whatever the world was going to throw at him.

His plan was interrupted by the sound of his ring tone, and Barker's Pavlovian response to it.

"Barker! I know you hate the Argyle theme. Anyone would think you supported Exeter City!"

He managed to swipe the green icon just before the messaging service kicked in.

"Tedesco!"

"Ah, John. Apologies for the early hour. Look, probably nothing…"

"Go on, Jos," said the detective, encouraging his friend to disclose whatever it was that had prompted the early call.

"Well, I was doing my daily circuit of the Close. I find it very mindful – it sets me up for a day of dealing with customers and suppliers."

"So I take it that something was different this morning?"

"Indeed. Look – as I said, probably nothing, but I noticed

that the Cathedral School's minibus was parked outside the school gates. Being curious, I took a closer inspection and saw that the key was still in the ignition."

His interest piqued, Tedesco muttered, "Go on…"

"This is where it gets really interesting. There was someone asleep on the back row of seats, so I gently tapped the side window. A man moved towards the door and delivered a most unsuitable hand gesture in my direction."

Resisting the urge to chuckle at Jos' trademark prissiness around displays of vulgarity, he let the wine merchant resume his narrative.

"I was somewhat unnerved, so I decided to report the matter to the school. But just as I was about to let myself in, I saw the man running at speed towards the Chapter House."

"I'm impressed. Ever thought of joining me in the agency? Seriously though, did you get a look at the man as he scarpered?"

"That's just it. He moved incredibly quickly for a large man, but it had to be him."

"The Neighbour from Hell! Thanks, Jos. This could just be what we have been waiting for."

*

Lady Derrington was also in a hurry that morning. She skipped breakfast, leaving her husband to his tea and toast and the *Daily Telegraph*.

She had an important meeting at Church House, and was convinced that she'd get stuck in rush-hour traffic.

When she arrived at the 15th-century building on

the far side of the Close which housed the administrative headquarters of the diocese, she was relieved to find that Paul Twigger had reserved a slot for her in the tiny car park, so she carefully reversed her Mini Clubman into its space, checked the mirror, and straightened her headscarf.

Then she removed a folder from the passenger seat and knocked on the ancient oak front door.

Twigger answered in person. He had obviously been awaiting Her Ladyship with a certain amount of trepidation.

She put him at his ease by deploying her practised charm. She was the wife of the Lord Lieutenant, after all.

"Mr Twigger, how kind of you to see me. Now, you must call me Fiona."

*

Over at Bristol University there was a growing restlessness in the lecture theatre.

Dr Walker was never late, but today she was keeping fifty third-year students waiting.

The faculty's student union representative, who was part of the group awaiting their lecturer, decided to find out what was happening, her first port of call being Carole, the faculty secretary.

"Don't ask me where she is. Perhaps she overslept," was her helpful response.

The students started to slow hand clap and some of them reprised the old classic 'Why are we waiting?', which got the attention of Peter Sills, the head of department, as he was walking past the theatre on his way to a tutorial.

Having been appraised of the situation, he tried calling

Steph on his mobile before asking the students to leave quietly, promising to let them know what was going on once he'd been able to speak to his colleague.

Sills was seething. Academics could get away with missing the odd lecture back in the good old days, but now that students were consumers there would be hell to pay.

Where on God's earth was she? Steph was the last person he'd expect to let the students down.

*

Keith Neighbour slowed down to walking pace as he approached the North Canonry and let himself in via the side entrance.

He went straight to the service flat, where he stayed when he needed to be in Rhyme, and showered and changed only after he had put a call into the Cathedral School.

The headmaster's secretary was habitually at her desk by 8am, so he got through to her straight away.

"Mr Neighbour! This is early!"

"Yeah, sorry about that, Deborah. Could you give Geoff a message? It's probably nothing, but when I was jogging in the Close earlier I saw that the minibus was parked outside the school gates. It had been left there unattended and the keys were in the ignition."

Deborah felt herself blushing. Mr Neighbour had that effect on women of a certain age.

"Of course I will. Mr Latcham will be in late today, but I will make sure he knows. In the meantime I'll ask one of the staff to move it back. I don't think it had been booked out yesterday afternoon – this sounds most odd."

"I agree – I reckon some unscrupulous chancer took it out for a spin."

As he ended the call, the chief executive allowed himself a wry grin. Not only had he removed himself from suspicion by reporting the incident, but the staff member's prints would also be all over the steering wheel. He, of course, had been wearing gloves.

FIFTY-EIGHT

"Bloody hell!" shouted Peter Sills. The normally urbane department head was clearly rattled.

"Why isn't she picking up?"

No one had seen Dr Walker since she left the campus the previous afternoon, and that was now twenty-four hours ago.

Sills decided to leave early – he could call in on his colleague on his way home: he still remembered where she lived as Stephanie had hosted a leaving party for one of the junior lecturers at the end of last term.

Arriving at the converted house in Clifton, he tried the intercom several times without success.

If she was at home with the flu, then surely she could have at least struggled to the door to see who it was, leaving to one side the fact that she would normally have called in sick.

He tried the ground-floor buzzer for a final time with no joy, but then the main entrance door suddenly opened and a bearded man wearing a pale brown leather jacket, a sort of retro *Sweeney* or *Life on Mars* number, emerged blinking into the daylight.

Sills approached him. "Excuse me. Do you live here?"

"Who wants to know?"

"My name is Peter Sills and I am a colleague of Stephanie Walker."

The man visibly relaxed. "Steph? I see. I live in the top flat, above her place. Is there a problem?"

"There might be. Look, could you spare me five minutes?"

*

Over in the splendour of Rhyminster Cathedral Close, Paul Twigger was having a hard time.

His repeated attempts to hide behind Keith Neighbour had met with stubborn resistance, and it was looking like game, set and match to Lady Fiona.

She had commenced proceedings by presenting the shy bookkeeper with a letter signed by thirty parish treasurers certifying that she was their authorised representative, politely requesting him to render whatever assistance Her Ladyship requested.

Too terrified to argue, Twigger accepted this at face value and then spent the best part of three hours being grilled about the invoices he had issued to the parishes.

"But, Lady Fiona, I send these out on behalf of Mr Neighbour."

"Mr Twigger. You are too modest. I'm sure you can help us. It's really very simple. We in the parishes don't have the depth of your financial knowledge. Couldn't you just look at a couple of these bills and explain what they mean?

"Now, this letter addressed to the treasurer of Wormley cum Penfold, for example?"

The poor man knew when he was beaten…

*

They wouldn't have known it, but Peter Sills and the man in the leather jacket, who introduced himself as Roger Holmes, were seated at the exact same table in the exact same café that Lynne Davey had occupied when she was observing Stephanie's movements a few days ago.

Sills explained to Holmes that he had been worried about Steph, as she had failed to appear at work and wasn't answering calls.

"When did you last see her?"

Holmes thought for a moment. "Yesterday morning maybe – yeah, I think I saw her picking up her post from the table in the hall."

"Okay, but what about last night?"

"I didn't roll in until the early hours of the morning. I'm a road manager for some local bands, so I'm a part of the night-time economy. I was over in Cardiff till gone midnight."

Holmes suddenly appeared concerned. "Look, mate, is there something up? Is Steph in trouble?"

"Not as far as I know. But you will tell me if you see her, won't you?"

They swapped numbers, and then Sills asked about the occupant of the ground-floor flat.

"Evie? You won't get any information from her, I'm afraid. Evie is short for Yvette, sort of. She works at the Arnolfini, but she took off early this morning for a long break with her folks in France."

FIFTY-NINE

Tedesco and Barker arrived at Minster Precincts just before Sally, who was busy unloading her usual array of jute bags from the panniers on her bike.

Just what did she keep in them?

The detective and terrier combo managed to enter the building without being spotted by the PA, and as they entered the cosy womb of 4a they saw that Lynne was already tapping away at the keyboard on her laptop.

She looked up, and greeted her colleagues enthusiastically.

"Hi, guys! Come and have a cuddle – that's just aimed at you, Barker, of course. John, you look like you want to tell me something?"

"Am I that transparent? Yes, I do have a bit of news…"

Once he had gone through the key points of his conversation with Jos Elsted, Lynne offered to call Jools straightaway as she remembered that DS Tagg was on a course in Truro later and would be leaving from home rather than going in to work.

"I should be able to catch her…"

*

Peter Sills endured a sleepless night, something of a first for a man who seemed to glide through the world untrammelled by worry or doubt.

He texted Carole, the faculty secretary, to say that he was going to be late as he had urgent business to attend to, and then he headed into the city centre, where he eventually managed to squeeze his huge 4x4 into a space on the top deck of the Broadmead shopping centre multistorey.

Google told him that it was a five minute walk to the police station at the Bridewell, and he used the time to rehearse his lines.

Entering the huge building, he somehow managed to appear at the front desk as if he had been teleported.

Trying but failing to disguise his irritation at being kept waiting while the desk officer dealt with a rambling account of a burglary in Fishponds, he checked his messages until he was called to the front .

The officer on duty was in fact a civilian called Ryan Penny.

"I have come to report a missing person."

"I see, sir, and how long has this person been missing?"

The hapless Ryan tried without success to persuade Sills that twenty-four hours was normally too short a time to raise serious concerns and so he handed the matter to the first available officer, Sergeant Keiron Forbes, who, assessing that 'we have a right one here', led the senior academic into a side office.

"This isn't a run of the mill disappearance, officer. Stephanie Walker just isn't the type of person to vanish into thin air."

"I'm not convinced that there is a 'type' who goes missing, sir. Look, have you contacted her family, friends?"

"Her blood relatives live in Australia and her husband was brutally murdered. You may have heard about it – the Bishop of Rhyminster!"

Forbes hadn't been expecting that; he allowed Sills to continue, while he took this in.

"So, officer, Stephanie is in a vulnerable state of mind. I really think that you need to be taking this seriously!"

The late Bishop James Provan was by far the highest profile case that the force was dealing with, so Forbes adopted a more conciliatory tone and promised to escalate the matter of the missing lecturer to the very top.

"And you will let me know what steps are being taken?"

"You have my word, sir. And in the meantime, could you let me know as much as you can about Ms Walker?"

After thanking Sills for sharing what he had gleaned from the neighbours, Forbes arranged an urgent meeting with DCI Verena Hill.

*

Back at Minster Precincts, Tedesco decided that it was time to call the headmaster. As a former governor of the Cathedral School, he knew that assembly would be over and that Geoff Latcham would be going through the day's agenda with Deborah.

His recollection was proved correct, as he was able to get through to the head straightaway and report Jos Elsted's sighting of a large man running away from the minibus. However, before he could mention the Neighbour from Hell, Latcham butted it.

"Thanks for letting me know, John. But Keith Neighbour

has beaten you to it. He called Deborah on the stroke of eight to report the fact that the minibus had been moved. It is something of a puzzle, but I don't think it is a police matter, do you?"

As Lynne would be raising the sighting with Julia Tagg, Tedesco decided to leave it at that.

On the other side of the Close, Paul Twigger had spent the night in Church House. Having realised that it was gone ten, and that he had missed his last train back home to Newton Abbot, he bedded down in the staff room and, after a fitful night, he managed to raise himself in time to get to Superdrug for some toiletries so that he could make himself presentable before his colleagues began to drift in.

Any lingering doubts he had harboured about Lady Derrington and her supporters had been blown away once he had started to go through the financial records of the sample parishes that Her Ladyship had given him.

The poor man felt overwhelmed by the sheer size and complexity of what looked to him like a huge fraud against the diocese.

The 'special administrative payments' that Fred Pound, the treasurer of Derrington and Hillbrook, had unearthed looked like they could be the tip of a ginormous iceberg.

The accounts for the Leatside group of parishes made for particularly interesting reading. There were large amounts received from the Edith Mountain Trust, followed by some suspicious outward payments to 'Christians Live Limited'.

Although Twigger was retained, effectively, as a glorified bookkeeper, he was astute and savvy enough to make some simple checks.

The Edith Mountain Trust had been set up in the 1950s to

provide funds for parish projects. It had a large endowment and had been well run ever since its inception, or that had been Twigger's assumption.

However, when he tracked down the names of the current trustees they included Keith Neighbour and Stephanie Walker.

A simple company search revealed that Christians Live Limited had the main objective of organising festivals and concerts. The directors were named as K Neighbour and T Goodacre.

If the red warning lights weren't flashing already, Twigger noted that the company was registered in the Isle of Man and that there was a holding company based in the British Virgin Islands.

Twigger then searched against 'Soaked by the Spirit festivals'. There, hidden away on its home page, was the telling line 'A Christians Live production'.

What was he going to do with all this information? As his line manager was Keith Neighbour, the loyal servant of the diocese knew that he couldn't go through the normal reporting channels – and if the massive Australian got wind of what he had been doing he would be out of a job.

SIXTY

As soon as DCI Hill heard the name 'Stephanie Walker', she arranged for Sgt Forbes to be blue-lighted into her presence.

Uniformed officers were deployed to carry out house-to-house enquiries in the vicinity of the converted apartment in Clifton and the building's caretaker was soon tracked down.

Hill, and her regular sidekick DC Kyle Brooks, arranged to meet him on site.

The caretaker was a dour Bristolian by the name of Dave Corcoran.

He had seen nothing, didn't really have anything to do with the leaseholders, and demanded to see a warrant to search Stephanie's flat.

"I have reasonable grounds for suspecting that a crime has been committed on these premises, and, Mr Corcoran, there is an offence called obstruction…"

Corcoran grunted his reluctant assent and made a meal of slowly unlocking the apartment with his master key.

But it was Kyle Brooks who made the gruesome discovery in the kitchen.

Hill called for back-up, and an ambulance.

Nothing had prepared any of them for what they saw – a semi-naked body, with a letter 'A' tattooed on its back. Even Corcoran looked shocked, and he headed for the bathroom.

Having arranged for the flat to be sealed off, Hill sent a text to DCI Jimmy Bloomfield. He needed to know about this urgently as, Hill realised, this must relate to the late bishop.

Bloomfield fired his response back – "It sounds like a serial killer. Holy shit!"

In the coming days, the medical officer would confirm that the deceased had been 'expertly strangled'. The apartment had been thoroughly cleansed and there were no usable fingerprints.

The chilling lettering had been sprayed on to Stephanie Walker's back using a stencil. In that respect the modus operandi matched that used against the late bishop.

The house-to-house checks yielded nothing, apart from demonstrating the atomised nature of a society where people didn't know their neighbours. The resident of the top-floor flat, Roger Holmes, repeated what he had already said to Peter Sills. He didn't know when Yvette Durand would be back from France, and he didn't have any contact number for her.

Correctly recalling that Yvette was presumed to have spent the night of the murder in the flat below Dr Walker, Hill arranged for Kyle Brooks to visit the Arnolfini Arts Centre, where Yvette worked as a curator.

Wisely assuming that the HR department would hide behind data protection legislation, the keen detective started at the café attached to the iconic building nestled in the harbourside.

He'd looked at the website and had found out that Bush House was also home to students and lecturers from the University of the West of England, which explained the large number of young people queuing up for lunch.

Having steeled himself for a long wait, Brooks noticed a group of more mature-looking people entering the café. They looked earnest, as if they spent significant time in libraries.

He went for it. "Excuse me, do any of you know one of the curators, Yvette Durand?"

One of the group, a man with a grey ponytail who looked like he'd wandered in from Woodstock in the 1960s, asked who wanted to know.

"I'm Ty Pearce, an old friend from back in the day. Don't tell me, she isn't over in France, is she? Just my luck."

"Afraid so. You've just missed her. She flew to Bordeaux a day or two ago."

*

Tedesco cut short his chat with his sister. Nicky had sounded much more upbeat, so he felt a heel for swiftly ending the conversation when Sally popped her head around the door to tell him that DCI Bloomfield had turned up unexpectedly.

Nicky had at least managed to tell him that Chag's colleagues were seeking backing for a management buyout of Aspirational Cars and that her lawyer, Susannah Shaldon, had obtained a positive opinion from counsel on the issue of the bank's failure to insist on her obtaining independent advice when she signed the house over.

"That's great, Nicky, that really is, but I have to go. I will call. Love to Ella, and Barker says hi."

Bloomfield was swiftly ushered into the conference room, followed by Lynne.

"Are we being raided by the hit squad?" she asked.

Her former CID boss affected to ignore her and concentrated on fiddling anxiously with his bow tie.

"Look, you will see the news but this really is top secret for now. Not a word to anyone, not even Barker."

Tedesco shrugged, then gestured for the DCI to continue.

"Stephanie Walker was discovered in her apartment this morning by Verena. She'd been strangled. And whoever did it had sprayed that weird lettering on her back."

This stunned his tiny audience into a temporary silence.

Tedesco eventually spoke up. "So who would do that, and why?"

"Jimmy," said Lynne, "Stephanie was charged and put on police bail for the minor motoring charges, and then she gets bumped off. Bit of a coincidence, don't you think?"

"I agree," said Tedesco. "If she was involved in her husband's death then I think we can deduce that her involvement would have been limited to taking the packet to the festival and then driving away, presumably to try and implicate Sean or one of the other followers of Aelred."

"Yeah, because the packet contained the 'A' symbol on the banner."

"And," Lynne added, "don't forget about the deadly nightshade in the bishop's morning cuppa – she would have been the obvious candidate for that."

"Back to my questions," said Tedesco. "Who would kill Stephanie and why? The real murderer? Did he or she think she would blow the whole story to the police when she reappeared for further questioning with her lawyer?"

Bloomfield stood up and paced around for a bit, stopping to stroke Barker.

"Jools has filled me in about what Jos Elsted saw. Could Neighbour have taken the minibus and driven it to Bristol, killed his lover, as I assume she was, and then brought the vehicle back to the Close early the next morning?"

"I think he could have," Tedesco noted, adding that Neighbour had very cleverly reported the missing vehicle to the school before he had called the headmaster himself.

At this point Lynne gave her business partner a meaningful look, then made a suggestion.

"Listen, I have it on good authority that the Cathedral Friends are having their monthly meeting now. It should be winding up soon. As John knows, Lady Fiona has been looking into some possible financial irregularities with the church funds."

"Yes," said Tedesco, "and we think there could be clues hidden away in the weeds of the financial muddle that could relate to the bishop's murderer – and possibly that of his wife, if it was the same person."

"So what are you waiting for? Why don't you send Dolly Daydream out there over to the Chapter Office and see if Her Ladyship can spare us a few minutes?"

*

The Bristol branch of the investigation had got hold of the relevant passenger manifest, which clearly established that Yvette Durand had been on board the Ryanair flight from Bristol to Bordeaux earlier that week. She had checked in one item of hold baggage, which had been labelled with her onward address, a private house in Arcachon, a coastal resort not far from Bordeaux itself.

With the help of the French police, Yvette was tracked down, and she readily agreed to speak to DCI Hill on Zoom and to cooperate in full when she returned from her holiday.

SIXTY-ONE

The meeting of the trustees of the Cathedral Friends, a charitable body that raised considerable funds for the upkeep of the ancient building, was just breaking up when Sally Munks arrived.

Lady Fiona affected no sign of surprise at being invited to Minster Precincts, declaring that she had an hour or so to kill before meeting some friends for lunch in town, so it would be super to see the agency team. "I hope Barker is in today."

Sally wandered back across the cathedral lawns with Lady Derrington, looking around to see if any of her friends had clocked her being out and about in such elevated company. Once they had arrived at the office, Sally led her prized guest into the conference room.

"John, Lynne. This is a pleasant surprise. And Inspector Bloomfield as well! This must be important."

Bloomfield calmly explained the latest developments to Her Ladyship, who expressed shock.

"But how can I possibly help? I hardly knew the poor woman."

The inspector formed his fingers into the shape of a church steeple and then slowly collapsed the structure, a gesture that Lynne recognised as a sure sign of nerves on the part of her former boss and one that Tedesco found incredibly irritating.

Once he had concluded the digital gymnastics, Bloomfield responded.

"I gather, Your Ladyship, that you have unearthed some interesting discrepancies in the church accounts."

"Do call me Fiona," Her Ladyship interrupted, without in any way appearing rude.

"Rather more than 'interesting', I fear. Several parishes have found suspicious amounts appearing in their bank accounts, and then payments have gone out to companies that they don't recognise. Then one of the treasurers reported that he was still awaiting monies from a successful grant application over one year after the award was confirmed. Paul Twigger, the accountant for the diocese, a real treasure, has started to look into it all for us."

"Fiona has been appointed by several parishes to act as their spokesperson," Lynne helpfully added.

Making a mental note to contact Twigger, Bloomfield addressed the room.

"Hmm. Sounds like money laundering. This Twiglet fellow, I assume he works for Keith Neighbour?"

"It sometimes feels like we are all serving Mr Neighbour rather than the Almighty," Fiona said.

"Lady Derrington does have a point," added Tedesco. "Neighbour has more titles than a Soviet-era dictator. Chief Executive, Chief Operating Officer and so on. I expect he has awarded himself several more. Possibly medals as well."

"So we know where the buck stops," Lynne added.

*

The Zoom call with Yvette Durand proved highly useful. She had spent the night of the murder in her ground-floor apartment in Bristol.

"I had an early start the next day, so I set my alarm in plenty of time for my taxi to the airport. I took a sleeping pill and had a large mug of cocoa with it—"

Verena Hill interrupted. "Wouldn't there have been a risk that you slept through the alarm?"

Yvette smiled shyly. "No, it is a familiar routine. If Dr Walker is being visited by her boyfriend things can get very noisy between them and I can't get back to sleep, so I take something to help."

Hill raised a suggestive eyebrow and Yvette tried to resist a giggle.

"No, nothing like that. This boyfriend has a very loud voice. He is a large man, a giant you could say. Everything he does is just – noisy."

"And was this boyfriend there on your last night at the flat?"

"Yes. I saw him arrive."

"Good. And was there a disturbance?"

"I heard them arguing before I got to sleep, but this wasn't unusual. If only I'd listened more carefully! I might have been able to stop what happened."

"Listen, you must not in any way blame yourself. You have been very brave in discussing this."

"There is something else," said Yvette. "I was only just

awake and so I checked my watch – I had a good two or three hours to snooze before the alarm went off."

Sensing hesitation, Verena Hill smiled and said, "Carry on, Yvette."

"Yes, well, you see, I thought I heard something. As if someone was cleaning up, a kind of scrubbing sound. I was half asleep, so I told myself that I was probably imagining it. But in the light of what happened, I'm not sure anymore."

"This may be highly relevant, Yvette, so please could you think back to that night, any detail, however small."

"Of course. And I know how to contact you."

"Now, the elephant in the room. I am going to show you a photograph."

Hill had set up the photo of Neighbour so she could show it clearly on the screen.

Yvette's response was immediate. "That's him. I know it is."

The curator promised to make herself available to Hill upon her return to the UK, adding that she was dreading returning to the apartment.

*

Back in Minster Precincts, DCI Bloomfield and his civilian helpers went through the events of the last twenty-four hours.

Could the police call Neighbour in on the basis that Jos Elsted had seen him in the minibus? The Australian would deny it, of course, and would emphasise the fact that it was he who had reported that the bus had been moved.

Could the financial irregularities unearthed by Her Ladyship provide them with an indirect route? There must be a case for interviewing Neighbour about it, as the buck stopped with him.

"I'm not sure that would be a great move, Jimmy," said Tedesco.

"I agree," seconded Lynne. "Look, if you go in with your size elevens and ask Neighbour for access to the books, what do you think he will say?"

"I expect he will obfuscate, tell me that I need a search warrant."

"I disagree," said Lynne. "He will be sweet reason. 'Of course, Inspector, I will make our records available to you. I just need a brief time to collate what you want. As a Christian organisation we must serve the interests of justice', blah blah, yadda yadda."

Tedesco jumped in like an eager whippet. "I agree with Lynne. Neighbour will ask for a reasonable time to get the books together, just enough for some judicious editing."

"So I think you need to see Paul Twigger, before Neighbour has the chance to get to him," Lynne suggested.

On his way back to HQ, Bloomfield received a text from Hill. As a result of Yvette's positive identification there was, after all, a strong case for asking Keith Neighbour to assist them with their enquiries.

Hill invited her Devon and Cornwall counterpart to a Teams case conference later that day. Bloomfield jiggled his diary and accepted.

Meanwhile, Tedesco had accepted another invitation. Jos had secured some intriguing samples of Barolo and would appreciate his friend's expert opinion. The former diocesan registrar agreed to be at Jos' place in the Close at 8pm.

"The invitation extends to Barker, of course."

Over at Church House, the Diocesan Office, Keith Neighbour was making one of his infrequent appearances to check in with the team, including his tame bookkeeper.

"How's it going, Paul?"

Twigger tried to look confident. "Just fine, Mr Neighbour. Receipts from the parishes are on target – do you want a look at the spreadsheet?"

"I can check on 'The Beast', but don't worry, Paul, that sounds great. Good job!"

'The Beast' was a computer program that gave Neighbour an overview of the entire workings of the diocese, including an instant snapshot of the finances. Only he could access it.

Twigger was only there for window dressing – or so Neighbour thought.

SIXTY-TWO

Why in the name of Ted Hastings did meetings have to be carried out on the accursed Teams? thought Bloomfield, as his colleague Verena Hill's sharp features pinged on and off his screen.

Despite the technical hitches, they were able to settle on a plan. Hill and the Avon and Somerset force would focus on the murder of Stephanie Walker, as it happened on their patch. Yvette's positive ID meant that they had enough to pay the Aussie a visit at the time of their choosing. Bloomfield and the Devon and Cornwall crew would concentrate on the financial investigation centred on Church House.

"I suggest that you call on Twigger as soon as you can, before Neighbour gets wind of anything and starts to cover his tracks."

"I gather from Lady Derrington that Paul is the anxious type, so I'll send Jools over with Matt Lovell."

After a quick stir fry for supper, Tedesco and Barker set off later that evening, pausing to admire the floodlit tower as they made their steady way across Cathedral Green to see Jos Elsted.

"They are using LED lights now, Barker. It's part of a green church initiative."

His best friend gave him a familiar, rather pitying, look so Tedesco upped the pace.

The wine merchant occupied a small one-bedroom apartment, which had once formed part of the teacher training college, which had closed in the 1950s.

Jos had decorated it with impeccably minimalist good taste, doing nothing that might detract from the enviable view of the south face of the tower.

Tedesco was, however, amused to note that his friend's sartorial appearance appeared to vary not one jot when he was entertaining, apart from a pair of blue carpet slippers adorned with a crest of some type.

It was probably a Christmas present from one of his growing fan club among the Ladies of the Close.

Jos greeted them warmly, and provided Barker with some expensive-looking treats from the market before leaving the room, returning with a bottle of the Barolo, a 2018 Patrizi.

A bemused border terrier looked on as the two friends sniffed and swirled to their heart's content.

"Well, John?"

"The notes on the bottle are in Italian, of course, but I think it describes the wine as robust yet ethereal. Sounds about right."

"I was thinking – maybe a bit strong for the Christmas turkey, but worth a shot with beef."

"Oh yes, an organic joint from that place near Totnes."

If Barker could talk, his expression suggested that the words 'what a pretentious pair of self-satisfied smug gits' would have sprung forth from his lips.

As the level on the bottle began to make its inexorable way to the bottom, Jos brought up a new topic.

"John, things are going well down here, to the extent that I am thinking of taking a tenancy of some premises. You have your ear to the ground and I am sure you could spot any obvious issues with the lease."

"That's very kind of you, but I would still recommend that you take full advice. I am rapidly getting out of touch with my old work.

"But hold on a minute – I've had an idea. I might just be able to help you."

Jos looked up at his friend with keen anticipation. He really did remind Tedesco of Paddington Bear.

"The tenant below us is moving out."

"What, the lovely chiropractor?"

"Tracey Webb, that's right. But it isn't widely known. She needs to expand to somewhere with car parking, so she's looking at Leatside."

"I won't breathe a word. Is it being advertised yet?"

"I doubt it – look, why don't I have a quiet word with her? It could be ideal."

Once safely reinstalled in his cosy bolthole in St Budeaux Place, Tedesco, half a bottle of Barolo down, found himself waiting at that familiar crossroads between melancholy and sadness.

He snuggled down in the den, where he was joined by Barker.

It was really happening. Lynne was going to Bristol. Sorcha was dead and Barker was getting older. How was he going to cope without them all? And what about his sister? Would she stay close at hand once the divorce had been finalised?

He went through his albums and, as he couldn't decide between two mood appropriate tracks, he played 'Empty Chairs' by Don McLean, followed by 'Lost Again' by Clifford T Ward, in each case savouring the intense pleasure he got from lining up the needle before carefully guiding it into the verdant valleys of the black vinyl.

*

The next morning, after a swift briefing from Bloomfield, Julia Tagg and Matt Lovell were on their way to Church House to interview Paul Twigger.

Jools had called ahead, pretending to be an anxious parish treasurer who wanted an urgent meeting with the chief executive.

Having got the answer she wanted – "Mr Neighbour isn't expected in today" – she correctly assumed that Twigger would be chained to his desk.

Upon their arrival at the jumbly, crenelated listed building, Candy, the cheerful Church House receptionist, expressed absolutely no surprise at being approached by two CID officers and calmly asked them both to take a seat while she went to fetch Mr Twigger.

When the sheepish bookkeeper somewhat reluctantly put in an appearance, Jools felt that she knew the type straightaway. Loyal to a fault, more than a bit institutionalised, his moth-eaten jumper suggesting a bachelor with a passion for bell-ringing.

What neither she nor Matt had anticipated was the eagerness, relief even, with which their visit was greeted as Twigger led them into his file-strewn office on the second floor.

"It may help if I tell you that I was expecting a visit. Lady Derrington tipped me off, as it were."

"I'm so sorry, sir," said Lovell. "She had no business in saying that."

Twigger put one elbow on the desk, then formed a cradle with his hand upon which he rested his head.

"I'm glad she told me. It gave me time to collect my thoughts and to collate what you need, although I fear that it may be the tip of the iceberg."

He removed his head from its docking station and sat up straight.

Looking pleadingly at DS Tagg, he said, "I'm not going to be interviewed under caution, am I?"

Tagg glanced at Lovell, who responded by reassuring Twigger that he was just helping with enquiries but that it would be appreciated if these discussions were kept private.

"And you may want to have a quiet word with your receptionist," Tagg added.

Twigger allowed himself a shy smile. "Don't worry about Candy. She is very bubbly on the surface, but underneath she is the very soul of discretion."

Then he summarised what he had told Her Ladyship, Tagg raising a quizzical eyebrow at the mention of 'T Goodacre' as one of the directors of Christians Live. Tim Goodacre had been the surprise witness who had given Verena Hill the scrap of the banner bearing the letter 'A'. It must be the same person, surely?

*

Bloomfield was already lying in wait when his colleagues returned to the Bristol Road HQ, decisiveness personified.

"Okay, well done. Lots to go on. We need to tell the Fraud Squad, they'll get the necessary production orders and the forensic accountants will soon be devouring the parish records like ants in a slurry pit."

Meanwhile, Julia Tagg decided to carry out her own side investigation, googling the Christians Live website.

As well as the obligatory five-star reviews and evangelical hype, she found brief profiles of the directors, complete with photographs.

Hadn't Verena Hill described Tim Goodacre as young, fresh-faced even?

So who was the mysterious Mr Trent Goodacre whose craggy features were revealed in the photo?

SIXTY-THREE

Jools popped her head around the door of Bloomfield's office. "Sorry to interrupt – but I think you should see this."

Preliminary enquiries had revealed that Trent Goodacre was a South African who had served in the apartheid-era military before beginning a chequered career as a 'security consultant', which appeared to have been a cover for recruiting mercenaries.

"Sounds like a top bloke," said Bloomfield, who fussily fiddled with his bow tie before suggesting that with a CV like that Goodacre would make an excellent cathedral sidesman.

"Maybe not mention that to Dean Dan?"

"Yeah, he might not see the funny side. Great work, Jools, but it was Tim Goodacre who was on Verena Hill's radar, not Trent."

"I was coming to that. I've been in touch with Avon and Somerset. Tim Goodacre checked out and he has no record. But he was born in South Africa…"

"So Trent is his dad?"

"No, his uncle. Much older than his father."

"Wowser," said Bloomfield, to his colleague's general astonishment. Not a word he had used before.

"But," the dapper DCI went on, "how come Trent got into bed with Keith Neighbour?"

"I'm looking into it, but don't forget that Keith was a marine before he joined Ocker Walker and his media empire."

"So he may have come across Goodacre on a training exercise, do you think?"

"Not sure, sir. My hunch is that Trent tried to recruit Neighbour as a mercenary. Ex-marines would be a likely target."

"And a rather large one in Keith's case. Okay, Jools, keep digging, and I'll report back to Verena."

*

In Bristol, DCI Hill was conferring with her protégé, DC Kyle Brooks. Brooks radiated eagerness, his shiny skin tone reflecting an outdoor lifestyle, in his case a mixture of surfing and rugby.

"We need to interview Neighbour as a matter of urgency. If he thinks we are on to him he could be halfway back to Australia by now," said Hill.

"I agree, ma'am," said Brooks. "But have we got enough to go on?"

Hill got up and stood on one leg, like a flamingo.

Sensing her colleague's puzzlement, she patiently explained that standing on one leg improved balance and reduced the likelihood of suffering falls in later life.

"Oh, and it helps me think. Listen, we have Jos Elsted's positive identification of Neighbour in the Cathedral

School minibus and that he saw him scarper when he was recognised."

"Granted, but Neighbour will deny it."

"Of course he will. But we have Yvette's Zoom interview, which she will confirm when she makes her formal statement. She can place him in Stephanie's flat on the night of the murder. And she heard them arguing, and then she thought she heard clearing up going on in the early hours."

"But isn't this circumstantial? She didn't see anything, did she?"

"Come on, DC Brooks, think about it. How many offences are committed out of plain sight? We have the suspect at the scene, a possible getaway vehicle…"

"What about motive?"

"Okay, what if Neighbour was behind the death of Bishop James and Stephanie was about to blab? Wouldn't that be enough? She would have been spooked by the number plate charges, and I can see her turning to Neighbour for help."

"So where do we go now, ma'am?"

DCI Hill reverted to a two-legged stance.

"I think it's time to pay a visit to little old Rhyminster. And as Jimmy Bloomfield has questions of our mate Keith as well, I will suggest a joint approach."

Bloomfield was amenable to the suggestion as he would welcome the chance to update his colleague in person on the Goodacre family's sudden emergence as potential actors in one or both of the murder investigations, as well as the growing financial scandal emanating from Church House.

Having established from Candy, the Church House receptionist, that Mr Neighbour would be back at his desk the following morning – "But he has a full schedule of meetings in the diary" – Bloomfield and Hill agreed to meet at 8am the next day. Brooks tried to hide his disappointment at not being invited.

Meanwhile, Keith Neighbour, the type of guy who kept several cell phones, was using one of them to talk to his old pal Trent Goodacre.

"I suggest you stay put over there till this blows over. Listen, mate, the local cops have got nothing to go on. The guy who works the night clubs was going to be out until the morning, the pretty little French bit of skirt was due back home in France before I got to Steph's place and the only bloke who saw me with the minibus was that gay wino, Elsted. And guess who reported the vehicle as missing in the first place?

"Yeah, spot on my friend. It was me."

SIXTY-FOUR

Back at Minster Precincts, Tedesco reflected on the call he had taken from Nicky before he and Barker had made their familiar perambulation through the most perfect open space in England.

It was great to hear his sister so excited. The management buyout was looking likely to become a reality and he felt rotten for having expressed his lawyerly scepticism when she first mentioned it.

Upon reflection, he realised that Aspirational Cars was a sought-after brand, and that if anyone could rescue that company, it would be Chag's right-hand man Geoff Pooley. If not exactly the brains behind the outfit, he was certainly the steady hand on the tiller.

As the bank appeared to be in the mood for compromise as well, Nicky was enthusiastically plotting a future using her share of the sale proceeds from Crane House to buy an apartment in a converted naval building at King William Yard in Plymouth.

"Ella will be at uni soon, Jack's left home…"

"So you can revert to your bachelorette days then?"

"I married too young to have any!"

He was pleased for her. Thrilled even. He'd dreamt of Nicky enjoying a Chag-free future. But, selfishly, he was going to miss her being only fifteen minutes' drive away.

And he was feeling side-lined from the investigation. The two investigating forces, represented by Hill and Bloomfield, seemed to have reached the stage where they needed little or no input from the agency.

Suddenly recalling his chat with Jos, he decided to see if Tracey Webb was around.

He'd never stepped inside her chiropractor's surgery, office, treatment centre or whatever before today, their irregular meetings taking place on the stairs or in the car park.

The reception area was unmanned, so he shyly knocked on the door to her office, where he found his fellow tenant of Minster Precincts tapping away on her laptop, perched on an exercise ball.

She looked up and greeted him warmly.

"How nice to see you, John! What can I help with?"

"Er, no, it's nothing, um, medical. It's about the lease to this place. You see, I know someone who might be interested in taking it over..."

*

While Tedesco was chatting to the attractive chiropractor, Hill and Bloomfield were hard at work planning their joint raid on Church House.

They would see how cooperative Neighbour was prepared to be on his home turf, but in all likelihood they would be asking him to accompany them back to the station.

Once he could tear himself away from Tracey Webb, Tedesco shared with Lynne his frustration at having been frozen out of the investigation.

"Self-pity isn't a cool look, Mr T. Listen, this may cheer you up."

Having shared with him Jools' conversation with her last night after their spin class, when DS Tagg had explained about Trent Goodacre, Lynne went on to explain that her former CID colleague had, in fact, asked for some more help from the agency.

Tedesco sat on the edge of his seat, keen to hear what this would involve.

Sally Munks, tactful as ever, decided that this would be the perfect time to ask her employers if they would like to sponsor her latest knitting marathon, this one designed to raise money for the food bank.

Having agreed to a tenner each, Lynne revealed to her partner that Jools had asked her to use her executive recruitment skills to approach Trent Goodacre.

"What! Is DS Tagg asking you to impersonate one of our clients and try and recruit Goodacre to some bogus job?"

Lynne kept calm. "Why don't you go and stroke Barker and then we can talk sensibly?"

Tedesco did as he was told, and then he admitted to feeling calmer.

"Okay," resumed Lynne. "What Jools is proposing is that I contact him on the basis that I have seen his profile on LinkedIn or whatever and that I would like to talk to him about some opportunities that might be on the horizon."

"I don't know. He's going to be suspicious, isn't he? And he sounds dangerous as well."

"I disagree. People – especially men of a certain age – like to have their egos stroked. And Jools will see everything."

"And how are you going to find him?"

"I'll start with his nephew. Tim. I expect he will forewarn his uncle that he may be contacted, which could work in our favour."

Jools had shared Tim's contacts with her and the eager young puppy was soon chatting to Lynne, who did her best to sound professional but with a top note of come-hither-young-man, older woman sexiness; whilst he was disappointed to learn that it was his uncle that she really wanted to speak to, he fell headlong into Lynne's toned-down suburban Mata Hari trap as he happily disclosed Trent's contact details, letting slip that his uncle had worked for a major Australian media magnate as his bodyguard.

The poor lad was putty in her hands as she ended the call with a breathy "Got to go, but hope we can speak again real soon…"

Lynne, using skills learned in the CID, had put a trace on Tim's number.

"I wonder how long it will take him to contact Uncle Trent…"

SIXTY-FIVE

As Bloomfield and Hill presented themselves at the reception desk at Church House, Candy's customary bright manner with unexpected callers was soon replaced with a wary anxiety when the two senior CID operatives showed their identification and insisted on seeing Mr Neighbour immediately.

"I need to call him first," said Candy.

"There is really no need. Could you show me to his office, please?" Hill said, assertively rather than unpleasantly.

The loyal employee nervously showed her guests up to Neighbour's huge eyrie at the top of the building.

"I'm so sorry, Keith," she began.

"No worries, love. I can deal with this."

Once the visibly anxious Candy had exited the stage, Neighbour coolly asked what business the two visitors had with him, warning them that he didn't take kindly to being doorstepped and that he had a particular problem with people who bullied his staff.

He spelt this out with menace.

"Are. You. Listening. To. Me?"

"How rude of us," said Bloomfield. "Allow me to introduce my colleague DCI Verena Hill of the Avon and Somerset police and I am DCI Bloomfield of the Devon and Cornwall constabulary."

"No, really? So what's with the antique-dealer look?"

Managing to control the urge to snigger at this, Hill apologised to Keith Neighbour for the interruption to his day.

"We came early so you can get back to your important work as soon as possible."

She glanced over to Bloomfield, who picked up on his colleague's cue and asked Neighbour if he could spare a few moments to assist with some enquiries.

The Chief Executive of the Diocese affected to look surprised before making an expansive open-palm gesture, then announcing, "Okay, no worries. How can I help you guys? Shoot."

Bloomfield shot a glance at Hill. They were on the same page.

"That's most helpful, Mr Neighbour. In that case, would you kindly accompany us to the station? We can be much more private there?"

Neighbour, affecting not to show any concern at this unexpected turn of events, asked if he was under arrest.

"Now why would you be worried about that, I wonder," said Verena Hill, as they led him downstairs.

"There's a fire exit – can we go that way? I don't want to worry the team."

*

Back at Minster Precincts, Lynne fired off an email to the lovesick Tim.

"Hi Tim, it was great speaking earlier. You've really helped me! Enjoy the rest of your day!

Lynne xx."

Having felt cruel as she pressed the send button, she then reflected that young Tim had tried to distract the investigation into looking at Silas, Sean, and Jayne when he had suddenly appeared at the police station with the fragment of the banner. The silly boy had it coming to him.

She then turned her attention to the uncle. Trent Goodacre would be a much more difficult prospect.

His naïve nephew had freely disclosed Trent's personal email address, as well as two mobile numbers and an address in South Africa. He had also let slip that he thought that his uncle was still in the UK – the clear implication being that he had been in the country recently, possibly at the time of the murders.

Using the email header that she used for her corporate work, and making sure that she blind-copied Jools in, she began to type.

She started by buttering up the potential recruit, telling him that his profile had been forwarded to her by one of her client's contacts, and that although her work was in the background of the recruiting process, she had become aware of a new position as Head of Security for a household name. This was highly confidential, but the employer had asked her to make an initial approach to ascertain whether this might be of interest. Emphasising the significance of the opportunity, she invited Goodacre to get in touch if he wanted to discuss this further.

As he was in the security business, and would probably suspect a scam, assuming that he even read the email, she gave out her real direct line number.

It was a long shot, but gambles had been known to pay off.

Over at Bristol Road, Neighbour appeared calm, insouciant even, as he sat opposite Hill and Bloomfield, rejecting their offer of a solicitor.

"I'm not under arrest. I've got nothing to hide. I'm just a good citizen doing the right thing – so why would I need a lawyer?"

"And we really are most grateful, Mr Neighbour," said Verena Hill. "Jimmy, I think you have some questions?"

"Yes, I do. Mr Neighbour, you worked for the late Bishop James, so you must have had dealings with his wife, I assume?"

"Sure. I have an office in the North Canonry, the official residence, so I saw a lot of Stephanie."

"And she is a fellow Australian?"

"She is, but where are you going with this? I've got a meeting with Pete, the temporary bishop, in half an hour, so can you get to the point?"

Verena took over. "Of course, we both understand. We are investigating Stephanie's death and so we are talking to anyone who knew her so we can put together a picture of who she was."

"And of who might want to silence her," said Neighbour.

"Understanding more about her background and her state of mind will, we trust, help us get to the truth, yes."

Bloomfield re-entered the fray.

"Did you know Ms Walker before you started your job with the bishop?"

"It's no secret. I knew her a bit. I worked for her old man. It's a matter of public record."

"Thank you, Mr Neighbour. And are you still in touch with her?"

"Yes, as a friend. I don't know if you are a believer, DCI Bloomfield, but as a Christian it is my duty to look out for friends in distress."

"But was it more than that?"

Neighbour's icy calm looked like it was going to melt as Hill stepped in, but not before she glared at Bloomfield.

"My colleague didn't mean anything, but I think it is reasonable to ask you if you had been to Stephanie's apartment as part of your pastoral care."

"And if so, whether you had seen her there on the day she disappeared?" said Bloomfield, who, realising that he was skating over ever thinner ice, swiftly caveated what he had said.

"Just so that we can eliminate you from our enquiries."

"Sure, I've been to her place in Bristol. But on the day she went missing – I don't think so."

Hill sat on the edge of her seat. "Thank you, Mr Neighbour. I do have one more question. You were seen at the apartment on the evening that we believe Ms Walker died, and we have a witness who claims that you spent the night there."

"But that's impossible. The other tenants were away, so who would have seen me? Not that I was there."

"Are you absolutely sure they were both away that night, Mr Neighbour…?"

SIXTY-SIX

Although he would never admit this in public, Paul Twigger was quite enjoying the attention as the forensic accountants pored over the books.

The Neighbour from Hell hadn't been seen at the office for a couple of days – nothing unusual about that, but Twigger sent up a silent prayer of thanks, nevertheless.

The ever diligent bookkeeper pointed the investigators to areas of concern, and it wasn't long before they were back in his office quizzing him about the Edith Mountain Trust.

He patiently outlined the aims and objectives of the fund and its underlying investments, adding that the current trustees included both Neighbour and Stephanie Walker.

The accountants, Don Record and Tricia Sullivan, went away again but were soon back in his office, looking about as animated as forensic accountants could get.

"Tricia has spotted something in one of the Mountain bank statements," said Record, who had the appearance of a minor clerk in a Henry James adaptation.

His colleague, Tricia – whose designer trainers, and

black athleisure trousers with a bold red stripe shot down each leg, indicated a passing acquaintance with the 21st century – thrust a copy of the statement in front of Twigger and pointed out an entry that she proceeded to highlight with a yellow felt tip.

The short-sighted bookkeeper removed his glasses and peered at the suspicious item.

'*Transfer to Goodie 2 Shoes Limited £200,000.00*'

"Does this mean anything to you, Paul?" Tricia asked.

Twigger replaced his glasses, then he slowly opened the drawer to his desk, producing a notebook that was a distant cousin of the pale blue counsel's notebooks that Tedesco used to write up his case notes.

"It's in here somewhere," said Twigger, becoming flustered.

"Don't worry," said Don Record, "we aren't in a hurry."

"Ah, phew. Here it is. I had been alerted to possible issues with the Edith Mountain Trust when one of the groups of parishes we look after, the Leatside Group, had received funds for a parish project from the Trust which they weren't expecting. Then the amount was transferred out again to a company called Christians Live Limited."

"We spotted the payment to Leatside," Record replied.

"We assumed this was a fairly typical grant award," added Tricia, "but if it was paid out again, then this looks like money laundering."

"I agree, I think," said Paul Twigger.

"But back to the transfer to Goodie 2 Shoes. I looked into Christians Live Limited – the recipients of the grant that was flipped from Leatside – and one of their directors is listed as T Goodacre."

The accountants looked across at each other, as if daring the other to speak first.

Don Record broke the silence.

"This may be a bit simplistic, but Goodacre – Goodie 2 Shoes? Could there be a clue there?"

*

DCI Verena Hill, sitting opposite Yvette Durand with her colleague DS Kyle Brooks, thanked her for making time to see them so soon after her return from France.

"Your identification of the photo we showed was the breakthrough we were waiting for. And I can tell you that we have a man in custody at the moment."

"But we do have a couple more questions for you, if that is all right," said Brooks.

Yvette nodded to signify her agreement.

Hill kicked off. "Yvette, did you discuss your proposed trip to France with anyone else – apart from colleagues and family, of course?"

"I don't think so – no, wait. I always tell one of the neighbours if I'm going away, usually Stephanie as Roger Holmes isn't at home very much. I ask her to put the bins out, keep an eye on the flat. I do the same for her."

Brooks joined in. "Very sensible of you. But think carefully about this. Did you tell Stephanie in this case, and did you give her a precise date for your absence?"

Yvette gave every impression of thinking carefully before she responded.

"I'm sure I told her, yes. But I may have given her my original departure date."

"Not sure I follow."

"I was supposed to have left on the previous morning, but I had to delay my flight for twenty-four hours. An important peer review meeting had been rearranged at the last minute and I couldn't miss it. Luckily for me, the airline could swap me over for the following morning without too much hassle."

"So," said Verena Hill. "If what you say is correct then neither Stephanie Walker nor her guest would have expected you to have been at the flat that night..."

Once they had finished with Yvette Durand, Hill called for Neighbour to be produced from the cells.

After his tacit admission that he just might have been at Stephanie's flat on the night in question, they had cautioned him and kept him in for further questioning overnight.

Unsurprisingly, Neighbour had requested that he had his solicitor present before any further questions were put to him, and so he was soon giving instructions to his lawyer, the high-profile Paula Fordham, who had been hired by Richard Swain in an earlier notorious murder investigation centred on Rhyminster and its ancient cathedral.

Fordham was still with him when he was called for interview, and she advised him to take her cue and not to comment if she looked up at him after a question had been raised.

Having reminded him that he remained under caution, and after introducing his lawyer for the benefit of the tape, Hill commenced by asking him again if he had been present at Stephanie Walker's apartment on the night she died.

Paula Fordham looked at him very pointedly, and he replied, "No comment."

Brooks tried a supplementary: "We have reason to believe that you were present in Ms Walker's apartment that night and that both of you thought that the flats above and below hers were vacant. Would you care to comment?"

"No."

"Okay, Mr Neighbour. This is getting a bit tedious. Let me cut to the chase," said Verena Hill.

"The flat above is owned by Roger Holmes and you correctly assumed that he would be out until at least the next morning. Yvette Durand, the tenant of the flat below, had informed Stephanie that she would be going to France that day.

"But what Ms Walker didn't know, and therefore you wouldn't have known either, is that Yvette was in the flat that night and she heard you both arguing."

Neighbour lost his cool, and ignoring his counsel's panicked urgings for him to shut up, yelled at Hill.

"She couldn't have been there! She was in France! She told Steph!"

"But she had to postpone her flight by twenty-four hours, Mr Neighbour. And so not only did she hear you arguing – nothing unusual about that from what she told us – but she heard you banging around in the early morning as if you were clearing something up. I don't know, a crime scene maybe."

"Keep quiet, Keith," said Paula Fordham.

"Okay, I think we have heard enough," said DCI Hill, sounding for all the world like Lord Sugar before he announces who he is going to fire from the boardroom.

"Keith Neighbour. I am charging you with the murder of Stephanie Dawn Walker. You are already under caution but I remind you that you do not have to say anything. But it may harm your defence if you do not mention when questioned something you later rely on in court. Anything you do say may be given in evidence."

The defendant was taken to the magistrates' court the following morning, where he was denied bail due to the serious nature of the offence and was remanded in custody pending committal to the Crown Court.

SIXTY-SEVEN

Goodie 2 Shoes Limited was a security company registered in Alderney with corporate directors. Further detailed investigation revealed a complex web designed to conceal the real people behind the company, but Don Record was not known in forensic accounting circles as 'The Terrier' for nothing, and he and Tricia were eventually able to unmask Goodacre and Neighbour as the beneficial owners.

So why was a security company being paid a large capital sum from the endowment of a charity that boasted as one of its trustees an individual, Keith Neighbour, who had an interest in the said company?

*

Back at Minster Precincts, Tedesco had just finished a particularly difficult interview with a potential client who suspected her husband of having an affair with one of her best friends. It was a difficult interview because the woman he had just seen was one of the Ladies of the Close, as was her friend.

"Come on, Barker, it's Jenks time." The walk to his favourite bakery would, as well as giving them both a welcome stretch of their legs, afford him some thinking time outside the four walls of the office.

This woman was asking him to keep tabs on her husband and his assumed mistress. He hated this type of work at the best of times, but he was torn on this matter.

On the one hand, he could charge what he liked in this case.

"Money is no object, Mr Tedesco," the lady had said. The agency could do with a huge fee, especially if Lynne was leaving Rhyme. Sure, she had said that she would work remotely, but the business of the agency was based on personal contact.

But on the other hand, the size of the fee was offset by the fact that the parties involved all lived in the Close, so he would be skulking around on his own doorstep. It would be next to impossible to avoid being seen. And anyway, the last place to conduct an affair would be within the ancient liberty of the Close, wouldn't it?

All of the residents knew each other's business there, or so he had always assumed.

After a pleasant haggle with Joan, he emerged from the bakery with a coronation chicken focaccia and a cheese straw. He liked a cheese straw.

Once he had picked up his paper from Smiths, he became aware of how many blank faces there were among the day's random pedestrians. He would check his diary later – perhaps it was International Idiot Day, or some such thing.

Having made it back to the safe harbour of his desk, he had just hunkered down with the easy crossword when Lynne powered up the stairs.

"Big news! They've charged Keith Neighbour with Stephanie's murder!"

"About time! Was Jos' evidence helpful?"

"I'm sure it was, but this is good, isn't it?"

"Of course. Perhaps they can pin the bishop's murder on him now. After all, they've got what I unearthed up in Helmsley."

Seeing his colleague look puzzled, Tedesco elaborated.

"The stencils, yes? And Avril, the lady who remembers selling them – she was pretty certain that the man she saw was him."

"And that 'A' shape was found on Stephanie's body as well."

Tedesco nodded, and got up and stretched before continuing the conversation.

"How are things with your financial investigation? This must all be linked, surely?"

"I haven't had a bite from Trent Goodacre, but the trace on his nephew's phone has come up trumps. The uncle has decided to pay young Tim a visit to his place near the docks in Bristol, so Jools has passed this to Verena as he's on their patch."

"So we may all be getting somewhere at last. Can I bring you back down to earth? How do you fancy looking into a ménage à trois in the Close?"

*

Verena Hill considered what to do with the intelligence that Trent was meeting his nephew round the corner from her office later that day.

What possible reason had she got for intercepting the meeting? On paper, Tim Goodacre had assisted the police with their enquiries into the bishop's murder by producing the fragment from the banner. Although this now looked like it might have been a diversionary tactic designed to throw suspicion on others, she only had supposition and an old-fashioned hunch to go on at this stage of the investigation.

And what did they really have on Trent Goodacre? Julia Tagg from Devon and Cornwall had briefed her on Lynne Davey's investigation into his background, which was interesting to say the least. The forensic accountants hadn't completed their work, so she was not yet aware of Trent's possible links to the fraud against the church. She decided to send a couple of uniforms down to the harbour to keep a weather eye on things.

Tim's work as a graphic designer meant that he could work from home, so he was able to meet his uncle in the late afternoon.

Trent didn't mess about. As soon as Tim opened the door, his uncle had him in an armlock.

"I came up here to see you in person. What the hell are you doing talking to Lynne Davey?"

"You are hurting me! She seemed really nice and the job she mentioned sounded like a great opportunity – didn't it?"

"You stupid dick. Weren't you even at least a bit suspicious? Turns out that nice Lynne used to be with the CID, and now she's part of a detective agency who seem to specialise in strange goings-on in cathedrals. So why don't you get back to her, tell her we've spoken and that I don't need her help. Got it?

"Oh," he added, "I don't have to remind you that you are on the radar as well. You did an okay job acting the innocent with the mystery package at the festival, but it would be wise to keep your head down. Our Australian friend has been disappeared and I wouldn't want the same for you."

Trent decided to release Tim from his iron grip.

"I understand," said Tim, between deep breaths, "so where are you going next?"

"Just jog on, Tim, jog on."

The uniforms had taken the number plate details for Trent's vehicle and they radioed in to report that the subject had left the property and was heading out of town towards the M4.

Later sightings showed Goodacre's SUV heading towards Southampton, where he picked up the M27, exiting at the airport junction. He boarded a plane to Alderney.

SIXTY-EIGHT

DCI Hill was becoming increasingly frustrated by Neighbour and his lawyer. Although he had all but admitted that he was present in the flat on the night of Stephanie's murder, the Chief Executive of the Diocese of Rhyminster denied any knowledge of the incident, brushing aside Yvette Durand's evidence as being self-serving. She had been friendly with Stephanie and was jealous of his relationship with her.

It was looking increasingly like he was going to enter a not guilty plea, despite his failure to answer Hill's pertinent question: if he didn't do the act, who did, as no one else had been in the flat that night? He also chose to ignore Jos Elsted's direct evidence of the stolen minibus.

Neighbour had wanted to hire Raj Purbani, KC, as his barrister, but as Purbani was also the MP for Rhyminster, the ambitious politician recused himself as it would be inappropriate for him to act in a case with wide constituency ramifications.

Paula Fordham secured him another top lawyer from a London chambers and, despite advice to at least consider a guilty plea as this could result in a reduced sentence, the

Neighbour from Hell dug in – until shortly before he was due to enter a plea at the next hearing.

The forensic accountants had been thorough. Their report would later state that this was one of the largest frauds carried out against a charitable organisation in the UK. The key to unlocking this had been the discrepancies in the accounts of the Edith Mountain Trust, which, as Paul Twigger had predicted, turned out to be the tip of a huge iceberg.

A warrant was issued for Goodacre's arrest and Neighbour would be interviewed under caution in prison.

Hopping over to the Channel Islands had proved to have been a bad move on Goodacre's part. Alderney was difficult to reach, but equally difficult to leave in a hurry, especially if Channel fog set in.

The South African had flown over there to meet with his accountants, who had set up Goodie 2 Shoes and various other companies and then registered them in the tax haven.

The £200,000, which he claimed had been a 'special dividend', had mysteriously made its way into one of his private accounts.

Under pressure, and realising that he had nowhere to go, Goodacre admitted that he had carried out some work for Neighbour. The work turned out to be fulfilling a contract to kill the Bishop of Rhyminster.

He wanted a deal. He would spill the beans on the fraud conspiracy in return for the Crown prosecutors acknowledging his cooperation when his case came to court. That plus credit for a guilty plea for the murder should see him out in time to enjoy some final years in the sun.

Once Trent had made his admission, the tower of dominoes began to collapse.

Having been charged with new offences of conspiracy to murder, fraud, theft and money laundering, down to a mixture of Goodacre's testimony and that of the forensic accountants, Neighbour decided that he had no choice but to cooperate.

His subsequent statement led to the arrest of Tim Goodacre for aiding and abetting the murder of Bishop James.

Neighbour pleaded guilty on all counts, including the murder of Stephanie Walker. The judge gave him credit for his guilty pleas and for his detailed statement, but he still received a lengthy custodial sentence.

Sometime later he was moved to HMP Ford, where he began work on his life story.

Trent Goodacre was given fifteen years and he served the major part of his sentence in South Africa. Tim got off relatively lightly, with a two-year suspended sentence, the judge deciding that he had been subject to considerable undue influence. He decided to retrain as a social worker.

SIXTY-NINE

Rhyminster, three months later

The aftershocks of the horrific murders of the bishop and his wife were still reverberating around the Close; indeed, the Church of England as an institution was going through a period of existential self-doubt.

Quite apart from the byzantine appointments system producing a candidate for the ancient See of Rhyminster who made Liz Truss look like the prudent choice as prime minister and the shocking lack of financial oversight that threatened to bankrupt one of the best run dioceses in the church, the way in which a malevolent outsider, in the shape of Keith Neighbour, was allowed to behave like a medieval pope had left the C of E facing calls for the archbishop to resign. Of course, it's habitual critics were repeating their tired old arguments about removing the bishops from the House of Lords with a renewed vigour.

John Tedesco, having paused his period of sad introspection while the investigation was going on, had plunged into a gloomy mindset once the drama and distraction it offered him had subsided.

And now here he was, cutting a lonely figure in the

cathedral refectory, wondering whether to go up to order another pot of Minster Blend.

His friends were worried about him. Barker sensed his master's mood and did his best to comfort him.

However, his human support network was fragmenting quickly.

Nicky's life was moving on at pace. The management buyout of her husband's business was agreed and Crane House had gone on the market.

Lynne and Duncan had decided to move to Bath. He could easily commute to the TV studios and she was eagerly anticipating a world of new friends, a decent theatre on her doorstep, not to mention a new and even more scenic Parkrun.

Duncan's promotion meant that Lynne didn't need to rush into finding a full-time job, so she repeated her offer to continue with the executive recruitment work remotely – but Tedesco correctly surmised that this wouldn't be permanent.

Someone like Lynne Davey would get plenty of exciting opportunities in a place like Bath.

He was beginning to question whether he should give up the agency, maybe retire. Do the cathedral guide training. Join the Sidesmen. God, he must be really desperate if he was prepared to spend more time in the company of Commander Foster.

Just as he was about to get up and head towards the refreshments queue, two familiar faces walked through the refectory and joined him at his table.

"John! Andrea told me I'd find you here."

Andrea Hutchins, the cathedral shop manager, had spotted Tedesco looking sorry for himself, so she had popped into the cathedral, as she knew that it was Canon Wilfred's turn to be in residence.

This duty encompassed looking out for signs of people who might be feeling lonely, who might have wandered into the ancient wonder in search of something to soothe them.

As soon as Andrea had explained the situation, the kindly precentor had texted Jos Elsted, who was free.

"If John's in trouble, then count me in. I'm on my way."

*

"Wilf, how good to see you. And Jos too! I was just going to order some more tea."

"All sorted," Jos said. "I ordered three more pots of Minster Blend on my way through."

"I thought it was about time we had a catch-up," said Wilf, "but why don't we try and avoid a certain subject, if we can yet."

"My thoughts exactly," said Jos, who had a different gilet on today. Rather jazzy, Tedesco thought.

"I wanted to see you both as I have some exciting news!" Jos went on.

"Another consignment of that excellent Barolo, I hope," said Tedesco.

The gentle vintner laughed. "It's even better than that. I've just been at the solicitors – your old firm, I think – and signed the lease on 4b Minster Precincts. It's just what I had been looking for. Tracey was lovely to deal with and she's happy now because she can move her practice into the new premises."

Tedesco smiled for the first time in quite a while.

"So we will be neighbours?"

"We will – partners in wine, and crime, perhaps?"

Sensing that his work was done, Canon Wilf slipped out of the refectory unnoticed, glancing back to see his friends laughing and joking together.

As long as there are still priests like Wilfred Drake, perhaps the Church of England isn't quite finished yet.

That evening, Tedesco's mood had subtly shifted from one of quiet desperation towards one that felt more like a kind of melancholy optimism.

Such a mood may not be recognised by therapists, but, as the detective poured himself a glass of claret and rifled through his vinyl collection, he found someone who clearly recognised the condition.

His musical heroes had never let him down, and this one had been with him throughout his life.

Time to hear the comforting tones of Mr McCartney.

The Beatles: 'I'll follow the sun'.

"Come on, Barker, bed time. I need to be up early to finish my case book."

Fin

AN EXCLUSIVE EXTRACT FROM:

To Hell and Back: the Keith Neighbour story

It seemed such a great idea at the time, taking the job with Bishop James. Great salary, lovely place to work, surrounded by idiots who couldn't tell a balance sheet from a wombat's backside.

Getting back together with Steph was an added bonus, or so I thought.

It only took about a month before I saw the chance to make some serious money out of the diocese.

There was no real oversight, and good old Jim Il Sung was too obsessed by his mission to save the heathen of Devon from woke Christianity to pay much attention to what I did. My old boss, Ocker Walker, was signed up to this blue-collar church malarkey, so I went along with it, rocking in the aisles at the happy-clappy gatherings.

Once I'd harvested more than enough dosh from my little enterprise I was going to be out of there. But then someone moved the goalposts.

One early summer's evening Stephanie lured me to the little summerhouse at the far end of the North Canonry garden. It was a lovely spot down by the river but completely private.

I should have smelt a rat when she produced a half-decent bottle of champagne. Her miserable old man wouldn't let a single drop of alcohol onto the premises.

He was out, as usual, berating some church folk in a far flung parish for their pathetic failure to meet with my success criteria.

After pouring us both a glass I felt her hand on my thigh. We had managed to avoid any physical contact since I arrived in the UK, but the attraction was still there.

"I can't bear living with James anymore, Keith. What are we going to do about him?"

"We? Hang on a moment. There's no we as far as I'm concerned."

"You may regret that. Didn't you know that I was a trustee of the Edith Mountain Trust? Or had it slipped your neanderthal mind?"

Steph had been through the accounts and noticed some, shall we say, not to put too fine a point on it, major discrepancies.

Let's cut out the boring bits of the conversation – the deal was that in return for keeping her trap shut about my profitable side-line, I was going to arrange for her husband to meet his maker.

And she wanted us to resume our relationship. As well as being a demanding tyrant, old James showed a distinct lack of interest in meeting his wife's most basic needs. Too much info, folks, but I put it as delicately as I could.

So, good old Keith had to act as a hired ram, commit murder, move in with a woman who he had fun with back in the day – but who wasn't what he wanted long term – or else his future would be ruined.

It took me seconds to agree to it. Money is my motivation and I wouldn't get a chance like this again.

Here's my little sermon: money is power, money buys respect. It means that you get to choose who you surround yourself with. Used right, it cuts corners. It gets you out of trouble. I love the stuff. I live for it.

So if I have to bump off the bishop and give his other half an annual MOT and regular service in return for her silence, it doesn't seem like such a bad deal, does it?

But of course, I wasn't going to be the one to bump him off, was I?

Do I look stupid? Don't answer that.

I know who does look stupid. It's those sad losers who go on peace marches, worry about so-called climate change, trans rights or whatever is flavour of the bleeding-heart month.

So, one fine day, as the usual suspects were protesting outside the North Canonry after Bishop Jim's excellent sermon, I asked one of those present what the significance of the letter 'A' on their banners was about.

It was a lightbulb moment. I could pin the blame for the bishop's unfortunate end on these woke idiots. They had plenty of motive, they really hated the guy, and they would be easy to manipulate.

Sean, who I identified as the lead hippy in the garden, was my first target.

I dropped in on him and asked to see the banner. His attempts to refuse were defeated by a classic from the Keith Neighbour playbook, the production of a packet of white powder backed with the threat of planting it on one of his unsuspecting mates.

Useful place, that Olde English Sweete Shop near the Close. It sells Class A sherbet.

Sean pointed me in the direction of a crusty by the name of Silas. We have a definition for his type back in Oz: *Lazius Bludgeratis, a common species found in the vicinity of employment offices or leaning on a shovel near road works.*

So Keith here paid a visit to Derrington Hall, taking care to make sure that Her Ladyship – an interfering old bag who I seem to have underestimated – was out of town, and I soon spotted Silas digging around in a vegetable patch. It was like the ones that kids get given so they can learn about growing their own plants.

And my, what was it that I found? Our old friend Atropa belladonna, or deadly nightshade as the likes of Silas would know it.

The leaves can get you high, which I guess is why Silas was cultivating it in his little garden. But if someone was to grind this up in a high concentration, it could lead to unconsciousness and even death.

The application of a minimal amount of force backed up with the promise to let Her Ladyship know about his little drug farm was enough to persuade our putrid mate to show me where he kept the banners and to cut out the letter 'A' from one of them.

Sean and his friend Jayne had already explained about Aelred when I met them on a fact-finding night out with the street pastors. Bishop Jim was keen on these types of groups – saving sinners, practical Christianity – and they told me about how they stencilled the lettering.

Another Neighbour brainwave. We needed to leave a calling card, making it clear that the murder was motivated by enmity to Bishop Jim's stance on our gay and lesbian cousins. What could be simpler than planting a clue about the old monk of Rievaulx?

No one I spoke to seemed to know where these stencil things came from, so, having looked into St Aelred, the patron saint of snowflakes as far as I could see, I drove up to Yorkshire.

I can already hear my Brit readers spluttering over their cornflakes – "You drove all that way, just to see if they sold stencils?"

Take it from Keith, a trip to Yorkshire from Rhyminster is like a little Sunday outing if you grew up in North Queensland. No distance.

And I didn't want to order online, even supposing English Heritage sold stuff through their website. Leave no trail, you see.

It was just my luck that the interfering pom Tedesco went to the same place. How should I have known that it was near where the old bishop had rested his hooves, and that he and Tedesco were old mates?

When I got back to Rhyme, the detailed planning began. Bishop Jim was due to speak at this huge Christian rock event that my company, Christians Live, was putting on in Somerset. This would be attended by four thousand crazy worshippers, so it would be the perfect place to ice the bish.

Sounds a bit callous? Grow a pair and get over yourself.

So who would I get to do it? Why, my old pal and part-time hitman Trent Goodacre.

Trent and I go way back. Old man Walker had used him for various top secret missions over the years involving phone hacking, evidence gathering and worse.

I had involved him in several little projects myself, including providing security for the live evangelical scene, and he happened to be over in the UK when I needed to call on him.

Trent was the kind of guy who had several passports and multiple identities. An ideal companion for a diocesan chief executive.

And he owed money to some impatient chaps in the UAE.

He haggled a bit, but we settled on £200k. I could easily lift it from one of the church funds then smuggle it away into one of Trent's network of companies.

So, logistics. I got Silas to grind some deadly nightshade into a powder and to deliver it to the North Canonry in a package marked for Bishop Jim.

I would, of course, arrange to be in to accept it, later claiming that I had no idea what the package contained and that I had simply placed it in the bishop's pigeon hole in the front office.

I would make sure that a generous teaspoonful went into the jar containing His Grace's special tea. As I had an access all areas pass where the North Canonry was concerned, I was easily able to do this before he appeared for breakfast that morning.

Steph had a little motorbike that she kept at her flat. She could hitch a trailer onto her SUV and so she brought the bike down on the Friday evening, where I transferred it into my huge vehicle.

This is where Trent's expertise came in. He had a nephew called Tim, who was fairly nearby in Bristol. Tim was keen and biddable, and Uncle Trent persuaded him to catch a train to Rhyme where he would be picked up and then once we got nearer to the site and the bishop was out of it, Tim would transfer to the motorbike where he would get to the festival and await a text from Trent before making sure that he was seen making a noisy and speedy exit from the festival office.

I'd already told Bishop Jim that I was giving a lift to a young festivalgoer, so he didn't question it when we stopped off at the station. By the time we got to the Trago Mills roundabout, Jim Il Sung was barely conscious. The belladonna, which seemed to have gone undetected as he chugged down his herbal tea, had done its job.

We picked up Trent at a services on the M5. The tight bastard had insisted on the money up front, so we had to hang around while he checked his banking app.

Trent took over the driving so he could drop me off about half a mile from the site, about ten minutes after Tim had transferred to the motorbike, which he would take all the way back to the North Canonry once he'd fulfilled his duty.

I already had my festival lanyard, so I could slip in quickly when I got to the entrance. I simply enjoyed the music, arms outstretched in ecstasy, until I saw the bike leaving the site. I knew where the cameras were so I picked a spot where I would later be seen in the midst of the crowd, just as events were happening off screen.

The ending came quickly for James Provan. He was completely unconscious on arrival, and Trent was able to get him into the fold-up wheelchair that we had borrowed for the purpose. Wasn't this difficult, bearing in mind how large Jim was? Trent was a killing machine and he worked out. It was a cinch.

I'd given him details of where the bishop's private yurt

was to be found. It was deliberately situated behind the main stage, and was further concealed by a high hedge.

Once he'd got him inside, Trent, wearing medical gloves, turned him on his front, expertly plunging the knife between his shoulder blades before going to work with the spray paint.

Later, Tim would be given the banner fragment and told what to say to the police, which should help to cement the connection between Aelred and the murder.

But once again it was Tedesco and his moll who threw us, when Lynne saw Steph on the bike and then recognised the kangaroo logo on the helmet when the cops came up with the evidence from the speed cameras.

That led to the unfortunate series of events that led to me reaching the inevitable conclusion that Dr Walker had to go.

It was the perfect crime. I'd checked to make sure that the neighbours would be out. Even when that puffball Elsted saw me the next morning, I reckoned that I'd disarmed any awkward questions by reporting the minibus as being outside the school gates in suspicious circumstances.

But just before my planned departure via Alderney and then to France, an urgent peer review meeting screws up all my dreams.

But don't feel sorry for me. I've kept my head down, been a good boy and I told the cops how I accessed the church funds. Thanks to Keith Neighbour, they've been able to recover most of what they thought they'd lost.

They should put a statue of me on the west front of the cathedral. It's the least they can do, the ungrateful sods.

This book is going to be a bestseller, and I've already sold the TV rights. Once they let me out I'll be on every daytime TV sofa in the free world, folks.

ACKNOWLEDGEMENTS

As a departure from the first two Tedesco novels, I wanted to use this one to explore, albeit on a broad-brush level, two very different visions for the church, and by extension, wider society.

The novelist and philosopher Ayn Rand has been a subject of fascination for me since I first read *The Fountainhead* as a comparatively young man. It's still a great read, despite the controversial views that come in its wake.

Rand, and her Objectivist philosophy have, in the intervening years, acquired contemporary relevance as the intellectual underpinning behind much of modern conservative thinking.

St Aelred of Hexham, Abbot of Rievaulx, is equally fascinating as his medieval ideas of mutual cooperation and brotherly love have been reinterpreted, some would say reinvented, for the present times.

It would be too simplistic to label Bishop James as a Rand sympathiser; she had no time for religion, believing that man's emotions needed to be saved from what she called the murk of mysticism – which I take to encompass religion – and to redirect those emotions at their proper object: mankind.

However, the bishop's particular brand of evangelical Christianity chimes with many who might be sympathetic to Objectivism, such as the media mogul Ocker Walker and his daughter Stephanie, who we see working on her series of essays called 'Ayn Rand: lessons for the modern Christian' while her husband is about to go on stage at the 'Soaked by the Spirit' festival.

Keith Neighbour could almost be related to Rand's hero Howard Roark – his 'little sermon', which I have extracted from his memoirs, could have sprung from Roark's lips – but Neighbour was at base a criminal with none of Roark's purity of purpose.

St Aelred's very different vision can be detected in the character of several of my regular 'C of E' cast, such as Bishop Bob and Dean Dan, but, having written three of these novels, I now realise that it is the precentor, Canon Wilfred Drake, who most closely reflects the gentle ways of the Abbot of Rievaulx.

And I think I am fairly confident on which side of the argument we would find John Tedesco himself.

I have an admission to make. One of the encounters in *The Turbulent Bishop* is loosely based on my own experience, one that shook me up when it happened, and which I have since had bad dreams about. Writing it into this book has been suitably cathartic.

So, has Tedesco reached the end of the road, or will there, as predicted by the Raven, be a new dawn for Rhyminster?

Have a quick look at the following picture for a possible clue.

In the meantime, thanks as ever to Lucinda for her loving support, and for producing the image of the friendly gargoyle, and to friends and colleagues old and new for their encouragement.

To everyone who buys, lends, or borrows these novels, I really appreciate it, especially in these straightened times.

Tedesco and Barker are most grateful.

And if you want to get involved in a wider conversation about my books, please do review them wherever you can, recommend them to your book club, or just talk about them to family and friends.

It is always good to hear from you.

Salisbury, spring 2023.

Radu Herklots has spent much of his life in and around cathedral settings. His grandfather was a residentiary canon at Peterborough Cathedral, and Radu spent the best part of thirty years practising law in Winchester.

He retired from full time legal work in 2019 to concentrate on his writing, and *The Turbulent Bishop* is the third John Tedesco Cathedral Murder mystery to be published, following hot on the heels of *The Cage*, which was described as having shades of Anthony Trollope's Barchester novels by *The Law Society Gazette*, and *Leap of Faith*.

He lives in Salisbury with Lucinda, where he divides his time between creating the Tedesco series and volunteering at the cathedral, as a guide and steward.